Her voice ~~[obscured]~~ he almost didn't catch the words.

"He hurt me, Erik. Oh God, he hurt me. Again and again. I lost count. Each time was worse than the one before. . . ."

He moved to her while she droned on. Her naked body was covered with grime, cuts, and welts. Her hair was filthy and matted.

"Then. . .in front of all those animals. . .the shame. . .I'll never be clean again." She lowered her face into the dust.

He knelt and cut the hide thongs. He stood up and said softly, "So what do you want? A medal?" Her body went rigid. "A St. George's Cross?"

The silence was thick and oppressive. Or maybe it was the smoke. She laughed deep in her throat. She sat up, flexed her wrists and tried unsuccessfully to wipe the grime from her face. She only moved it around a little.

"God, I'm sore. How long have you known, you bastard?"

THE HALO SOLUTION

RICHARD NEEBEL

CHARTER
NEW YORK

A DIVISION OF CHARTER COMMUNICATIONS INC.
A GROSSET & DUNLAP COMPANY

THE HALO SOLUTION

Charter Books
A Division of Charter Communications, Inc.
A Grosset & Dunlap Company
360 Park Avenue South
New York, New York 10010

2 4 6 8 0 9 7 5 3 1
Manufactured in the United States of America

To the Choker, without whom this could not have been written.

—R.P.N.

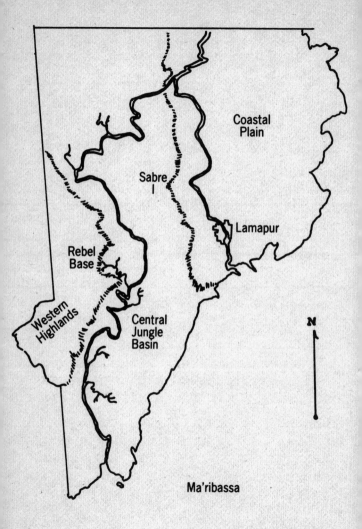

Coastal Plain

Sabre

Lamapur

Rebel Base

Western Highlands

Central Jungle Basin

N

Ma'ribassa

CHAPTER ONE

I'm a professional soldier. I fight when I have to, and very glad to get out of it when I haven't to. You're only an amateur: you think fighting's an amusement.

G. B. Shaw, *Arms and the Man*

He learned from recent interrogations that the Mpeche had given him a new name: Mloku-arambi-chlapaku, He Who Smiles With His Teeth Often But Laughs Never. The name was used to scare black children, and many young warriors wished to drink his blood, eat his heart, and thus acquire his prowess.

Erik Chatham was his given name. He maintained that he was just a simple country boy, born and bred. But that would be a little hard to explain to a hopped-up black bastard in the middle of the bush. Not that he'd ever take the time. The more lies the ju ju men sang about him, the better. At worst, it could only make the warriors hate him a little more than they did already, which was considerable. And at best, it might make some spearman hesitate a fraction of a second too long. His life expectancy had been based on those fractions quite a bit lately.

Going by the war songs, the spearman probably wouldn't recognize Chatham if he did stumble over him. Granted, whites generally are larger than the starving, diseased Mpeche. But Chatham didn't come near being the seven feet tall the witchmen maintained. He was closer to 5'11" and though he was rather slim, he hadn't had any luck transforming himself into an adder that lies in the tree tops and drops on passing tribesmen. His dark brown hair could never be mistaken for white. But then, the tendency was to think of all Caucasians as being colorless. To hear them tell it, rather unflatteringly, Chatham's face was disfigured by dozens of battle scars. However, he did have more than the usual allotment of scars on his body, obtained painfully in the line of duty. But there was only one scar on his otherwise ruggedly handsome face, running from the corner of his right eyebrow halfway down the right cheek. That, he was almost embarrassed to relate, he picked up in an auto wreck just outside Stockton, Illinois, when he was seventeen. As for the pointed leopard teeth that drip with the blood of Mpeche babies, well, he had been told by some young ladies that his teeth were very attractive. He expressed mock concern that it was the only flattering thing they could think up on the spur of the moment.

He spent a rather nondescript twenty years as a

Midwestern, all-American boy. He was usually the kid who ended up without a date to the prom, and the only thing that kept him out of the ranks of the distrusted bookworm was an acceptable ability to play high school and college football.

A rather ordinary existence until Uncle Sugar made it obvious that he also had an aptitude for killing. The government provided him with the best book learning in the field at various Stateside posts and on-the-job training in Southeast Asia. When that term of employment ended rather hastily, he began his graduate work here in the Kingdom of Ma'ribassa. The line of work wasn't much different, but at least it was more lucrative.

In his officer evaluation reports, he had been described by a few sympathetic superiors as a practical soldier. This was a kindly attempt to mask the fact that he had no use for the deep study of obsolete military theorists and their tactics. He read and digested Clausewitz, Molke, and Liddel Hart, and discarded them. He was foremost a guerrilla fighter and, given the world situation, he wouldn't want for work. He read and remembered the lessons taught by Ernesto Che Guevara, the pseudo-Cuban, Nguyen Van Hieu, and the rest of the boys in the band. He usually remembered them better than their authors.

That's how, very briefly, Chatham came to be where he was: sitting in the middle of a jungle, painted various shades of camouflage green, carefully reassembling his machine pistol. It hadn't been used enough recently to necessitate the cleaning he had just given it. But the spare time maintenance of his tools had become a habit. He inserted the bolt assembly, replaced the receiver cap on the Sterling, and repacked the oily cleaning patch in his butt pack. On regular missions, he didn't use a silencer. They were clumsy and an added cleaning bother. He gently inserted a curved thirty-round clip in the magazine well. It was all very well for movie heroes to slam in clips with virile gusto. But he much preferred a weapon that functioned to flaunting his muscles. He worked the charging lever, switched the fire selector to safe, and moved to his four companions in a silent crouch.

It was impossible to tell them apart in the early morning darkness. The tiger camouflage jungle fatigues and bush hats were identical, as was most of their equipment. Features were obliterated by camouflage greasepaint that had been melted together by rivulets of sweat, mud, and stagnant swamp water. As Chatham moved among them, they looked to him from where they lay sprawled in the thick jungle growth.

Chatham's wristwatch read 0500. He motioned for them to move out. They got to their feet without a word, grasping their FN assault rifles. From the moment that a mission started in the bush, words were rarely spoken, and when they were, they were whispered. Their lives depended not on traveling through the jungle, but on becoming an integral part of it.

The squad was made up of specialists. The rifle

companies of the 3rd Volunteer Territorial Para-commandos did their work in relative safety of numbers in massive assaults. Their continued voting membership in this world was insured by their expertise in killing. Chatham's unit depended on their expertise in unnoticed killing. The U.S. Army called them "lurps"—long-range recon patrols. Five-man intelligence squads, the sense organs of the regiment, were dropped secretly by helicopter deep in the enemy-controlled jungle to find rebel concentrations so that others could slaughter them. The missions usually lasted two weeks. Everything they needed—food, water purification tablets, ammo—they carried on their backs, sometimes eighty pounds of it. They didn't smoke and buried all waste before moving on. Many solitary warriors had died, covered in glory and drowning in their own blood because they thought they ruled their arena. The psychological effect of hitting the enemy in their own safe backyard was impressive. One night Chatham's men came on five Mpeche asleep by the trail. They slit the throats of three of them and didn't stay around for the survivors' awakening.

And Chatham's squad was good. Regimental Sergeant-Major L'Escaut had learned his craft in Algeria and Katanga, as had Corporals Rochereau, Dampierre, and the Belgian, Rifleman Gertewoute. The mercenaries, labeled volunteers by His Majesty's government, were mostly French, Belgian, or South African.

The unsavory family of jungles has many faces.

Chatham had seen three and hadn't fallen in love with any of them. He took his survival training in the Panamanian branch, then moved to the Vietnamese and Cambodian cousins. For its full measure of rottenness and filth, his present abode took full honors. Unlike some that just resembled untended, thick forests, the Ma'ribassan was a hothouse turned vicious.

They were lying in position at the north end of the village, about fifty meters from the outlying huts. The village squatted in the middle of a rough rectangle hacked and burnt out of the heart of the bush. It was large by Mpeche standards, having about fifty huts in varying states of disrepair. There were no streets. The huts had been erected where the occupants felt like assembling materials. These varied from dried cow dung and mud to flattened tin cans. The dung and mud dissolved in the seasonal rains and the tin cans began to rust away in the moist air the day that they were hammered together. The single unifying feature of the hovels was the traditional grass roof, harboring insects, lizards, rats, and snakes, each devouring the others in turn.

The reason for the size of the village sat in the center. The single-story mission hospital was constructed of white-washed baked brick, designed for twenty-five beds and containing fifty. The building held the dispensary, the sick ward, and the nuns' quarters at the rear. Their quarters had become their prison, and that was why the men were here. That was also why, at the south end of the village, there were three hundred Mpeche warriors drunk with raw native booze, bhang, and bloodlust.

Until yesterday, the squad had been miles away. Gertewoute's radio had crackled to life unexpectedly as they were combing the bush. Headquarters ordered them out after only five days in the lowland maze. Chatham transmitted the coordinates of a suitable landing zone and at dusk, they climbed into the camouflage-painted skin of the Westland Whirlwind. A major from Intelligence began the briefing as the chopper gained altitude over the darkening forest.

For years, the lowland Mpeche blacks had been chafing under the nonbenevolent rule of the Semitic Zakariya tribe of the coastal highlands. For centuries, the black tribal majority had been held subservient to the descendants of Arab slavers. To further complicate things, there was the long history of British presence. The English still mined the vast mineral treasures of Ma'ribassa, virtually the only export of value in the small nation. English commercial companies had gained enormous wealth from the monopoly and, in return, bestowed riches on the Zakariya for allowing them to do so. Business as usual.

The docile obedience of the blacks had changed with the appearance of Mpanda Mhlangana. Rumor had it that the rebel leader had been trained in Peking. It might have been a myth conveniently created to soften criticism of the massive Western military aid lavished on Field Marshal Yusuf ibn-

Tashfin to ensure the freedom of the law-abiding citizens. The Communist version would differ, but its doubletalk was worth as much as their opposite number's.

In the beginning, the rebellion had been scattered and impotent. The guerrillas were few and hard to find in the lowland jungle. Zakariyan soldiers did not like the steamy basin. They contented themselves with destroying the Mpeche villages at random, raping the women and killing the men. As the villages died, more and more Mpeche fled to the bush and the waiting guerrillas. The tide turned as the blacks became more proficient in killing the well-armed Zakariyans from ambush with poisoned arrow and spear. The fierce warrior blood of the Arab slavers had been watered down by successive generations of easy living. The more that died in the jungle, the more deserted and returned to the safe highland plateau. Field Marshal Tashfin needed soldiers who would fight. Experienced professionals are never hard to find if the pay is right. Tashfin stopped buying tanks with his foreign aid and began to buy an army.

Two regiments of "volunteers" were soon raised. The native army returned to Lamapur, the capital, to parade before the palace while the volunteers moved to the lowland outposts. The forces of freedom again began to destroy the Communist aggressor. But, with few exceptions, other nations did not approve of white mercenaries efficiently slaughtering uncivilized blacks. At least not in public.

Wars are painted in black and white. The Mpeche were being attacked as a tribe. Anyone who was not of the tribe was an enemy. Bystanders began to die. Fifty white miners and mining engineers died in a night raid on Complex 18, Britannia Mining Company, Ltd. Several days later, a Peace Corps school was burnt, killing the three U.S. citizens in it.

To be saleable, newspaper headlines must be recent and disastrous. Massacres drew correspondents to Ma'ribassa like flies to a corpse. The dictator had an eye for public relations, or propaganda, depending on your inclinations. Tashfin courted world opinion by a well-publicized rescue operation. Evacuation of the remaining foreign nationals was accomplished by the Zakariyan army with much fanfare and no bloodshed. The white man's outposts were given up to the advancing Mpeche. All except for the Catholic mission hospital at Zamboji. Father Beauchamps and seven nuns refused to be evacuated, choosing to stay and minister to their flock. The Mpeche came, took the whites captive, and sat in wait for the rescuers.

The briefing in the noisy helicopter was terse. There were no roads to the Zamboji Mission, only footpaths. Any large rescue force would sustain heavy casualties. If or when the force arrived, it would probably find the missionaries dead and the Mpeche gone. There was a clearing at the southern end of the village where supplies used to be parachuted to the priest. But sharpened stakes four feet long now obstructed the field. They could kill paras and puncture low-slung chopper fuel tanks.

Time was running out. The boss wanted good PR, but valuable equipment would not be risked on one priest and seven nuns. One rescue attempt and one only would be made. Chatham was told that his squad was the only one possessing the skill and courage to pull it off. He automatically translated that into they were closest. During the briefing, they were flown to another LZ five miles from the mission. A march through the night brought them to the river, where they rested until dawn.

While three choppers created a diversion at the southern field, Chatham's squad would infiltrate from the north. The balloon would go up shortly after dawn in hopes that most of the occupation forces would be dead drunk or busy with the diversion.

There were no better odds. But then, Chatham had rarely been offered better. They would be either be the Saviors of Zamboji Mission or they would be dead.

Crossing the stream in the half-light of false dawn had been uneventful. The unnamed, waist-deep tributary contained neither crocodiles nor leeches in any great number. They reached the assault point as the sun cleared the tree line. They stripped to fighting weight, checked ammunition and frag grenades, then settled down to get a little more rest.

For two hours the jungle fighters watched the village stir to life. Ground fog and cooking fire smoke turned the clearing into a misty pond with thatched boats. Warriors came out of the huts and relieved themselves before moving off to the south. Most of the enemy had slept among the stakes where they had fallen in a drunken stupor the night before. Now they were on their feet and milling around. Occasionally there was the glitter of the sun on a *seme* swordblade or a spearhead.

"Sergeant Major, what does the hospital look like?" Chatham whispered in English, the lingua franca of the small African kingdom.

"No guards posted outside, sir," L'Escaut whispered back without lowering his binoculars. "But I saw movement through the ward windows."

"Probably Mpeche. The hostages should be kept in the nuns' quarters. No windows to worry about."

The Mpeche heard the choppers before the hidden attackers did and became more agitated. Faintly, the *chut-chut* of the rotored turbine engines reached the whites. Three specks became visible to the south, skimming the trees. As they grew larger and louder, a low moan from the mob started and grew in intensity.

"Wait for the firing to start before we move out." Chatham smiled and wondered why he'd said it even as the words came out. If any squad wouldn't jump the gun, it was his.

The Whirlwinds reached the unusable LZ and hung suspended over its center. Arrows arched up at the machines, then fell back into the boiling black mass. The metal birds remained out of range.

The natives set up a howl of rage and frustration. Door gunners from all three choppers opened fire with light machine gums. Tracers rocketed into the packed crowd below, but no one ran for cover. Warriors fell, and those only wounded soon died under the calloused feet of their brethren. The ju ju men had made magic. Only those who did not truly believe would die. For the others, the white man's bullets would turn to water. They were probably told that they were the only squad with the skill and courage to pull it off, too.

One chopper darted lower, as if to land. The screeching redoubled and a second cloud of arrows rose. Most bounced off the metal skin, but some stuck fast. When the chopper returned to its safe altitude, its belly had sprouted whiskers.

"Now," Chatham said, and the squad trotted down the incline with weapons ready.

They spread into a loose skirmish line with each man just visible to the others through the smoky. mist. The pace slowed once they were among the huts. They continued firing from the helicopters and the roar of the mob grew louder as they advanced.

Chatham broke stride as he rounded a hut.

"Father Beauchamps doesn't need us now," Corporal Dampierre said quietly.

The priest's body sprawled in the dirt. His legs had been hacked off below the knees and two sticks had been impaled in the stumps. His white cassock was in shreds from knife slashes. His head rested about ten feet from the body, his severed penis and testicles rammed into the open mouth. A coat of shimmering blue-black flies swarmed over the parts of the corpse. Chatham motioned the paras on.

Passing deserted hovels, they made it three-quarters of the way to the hospital before they made contact. Coming around a mud hut, Chatham almost ran into a naked, painted black pissing against the wall. His bloodshot eyes widened as the white leader triggered a three-shot burst from his Sterling. The 9-mm high-velocity slugs struck the black full in the chest, and he crumpled like a puppet with cut strings.

Two warriors stumbled into the doorway of a hut off to the right and were cut down with a sweeping burst from L'Escaut's assault rifle. Chatham hoped that the noise of the shots had been drowned out by the continuing fusillade from the choppers.

The gunfire had forewarned a closer enemy. Chatham, on point, passed a tin-walled hut, spotting no danger lurking in the gaping black entrance hole. But his peripheral vision detected and tracked the hunchbacked shape that exploded out of the gloom. The Mpeche didn't waste time in straightening but zeroed in on the off-balance leader, crouched over the long spear shaft that he hugged tightly against his belly.

Chatham shifted clumsily to face the ambusher. His right foot slid out from under him on a clod of refuse. Chatham's brain shifted to stress-induced slow motion, and it observed detached from the cold horror screaming through his veins as the black death inexorably advanced. The brain noted the yellowed ivory eyes shot with blood, the spittle flecks blown past cracked lips and rotted teeth, and the pumping leg muscles covered with crumbling dried paint daubs. The spear point lowered, compensating for Chatham's uncontrolled fall.

The blow was like a sledgehammer in Chatham's under belly. It jolted the sluggish time frames back to normal speed. The added force slammed Chatham to the ground, raising a cloud of powdery dust. He gasped desperately for breath that wasn't there. The black grunted through clenched teeth and fought the upright spear still anchored to Chatham, trying to push it in deeper when he couldn't lever it free. Chatham squirmed on its point, flailing with his arms to recover the fallen machine pistol. The black abandoned the shaft, stepped back from his disabled prey and drew a rusted *seme* from a leather scabbard. In a two-handed grip, he raised it overhead, and for a split second shifted his gaze from his grounded quarry. Too late to counter the new threat, the black took the wooden rifle stock full in the face.

Rochereau had swung the clubbed rifle in an arc for maximum impact. The Mpeche somersaulted backward, his nose and cheeks a ruined mass of broken bone and gore. He was groggily pulling himself up on his elbows when Rochereau reversed the rifle and slammed its steel-shod butt plate into the vulnerable nape of the neck. The corpse collapsed like a steer in a slaughterhouse.

Chatham struggled awkwardly to his feet, fighting the alien growth of the spear. The point was firmly embedded in the metal buckle of his belt.

Having more luck than his late assailant, Chatham wrestled with the shaft, finally jerking it free. It was bent and gouged from the buckle, with fresh blood coating the crude but effective weapon.

There was a dull aching pain localized in the pit of Chatham's belly, and blood soaked his filthy shirt front. There was no time to check the seriousness of the wound or to ponder the possibility of poison. There was no place in the operation for incapacitated wounded. With no alternative, Chatham painfully retrieved his weapon and stumbled away, giving a wave of thanks to Rochereau.

The hospital loomed up and the invaders sprinted the last twenty-five meters. One of the nuns was tied to a post before the front veranda. She was part of the bait: the goat to attract the tigers. She had been stripped naked and sagged against the straps that held her upright. Her soiled veil, all that remained of her clothing, hung from her neck and fluttered limply in the breeze. There was dried blood on her thighs, gashes and scratches covering her upper torso. She had been gang-raped by dozens of Mpeche. Her three guards fell in a hail of bullets before they had time to aim their spears.

The squad ignored the helpless woman and ran for the building. They fanned out, L'Escaut, Gertewoute, and Chatham heading for the veranda, the other two for the side windows. As he reached the front door, Chatham could hear the chatter of automatic rifles and the shattering of glass. He kicked the door off its hinges and threw himself to the right, flattening against the outside wall. As Chatham cleared the line of fire, L'Escaut and Gertewoute emptied their rifles in sweeping bursts through the doorway. Chatham slipped in while they reloaded.

He scanned the dim interior. Two paces in front of him, sprawled in the dispensary door, was a black corpse lying on its back. There were no marks on the body and broken pharmaceutical bottles, pills, and powders were scattered everywhere. White man magic. If one pill is good, fifty are better. Chatham smiled at Father Beauchamps's posthumous revenge and looked past the dead man.

There were nine blacks amid the wreckage of the hospital beds. A few were down and still, but most rolled and crawled aimlessly on the blood-spattered floor. A few quick bursts from Chatham's machine pistol and all were still.

"All clear!" he yelled through the shattered windows. When acknowledged, he moved forward. He fed a full magazine into his weapon, aware that L'Escaut and Gertewoute had joined him.

Chatham kicked in the next door and dodged to the inside wall. He arced the muzzle of the machine pistol, covering the tiny room. There were no Mpeche there, only the women.

Five nuns huddled in each other's arms in a dim corner. Little was visible except the whites of their eyes and the remnants of the soiled tropical habits. Like cornered animals they moaned and whimpered, but remained perfectly still, like hunted rabbits. The tattered clothes, bruises, and scratches told of additional rape and abuse. The haggard faces masked the youth of the women. On a cot near the center of the room lay the unmoving body of an older, gray-haired nun.

One of the sisters, her prettiness showing through the pain in her face, ignored the intruders and spoke to no one in particular. "I think Sister Bernadette died of a heart ataack." Her voice was unnaturally calm. "They were taking her out to the mob and she just . . ."

"Come, we must go quickly." Chatham's voice was harsh as his laboring lungs pushed it past his raw, dry throat. He made a conscious effort not to touch his wound, afraid of what he would find. It must have been the English that stopped the whimpering. The trio's appearance certainly didn't foster confidence. Chatham motioned the rest forward. They lifted the nuns to their feet and herded them toward the door.

The speaker continued to ramble. "After she died, they were going to use her body anyway, but . . ." She seemed to notice Chatham for the first time. "We must take her body. . . ."

"Leave it. She's past caring." Even if Chatham had wanted to be less harsh, the young nun was in no condition to appreciate it.

"She died in a bad way," the nun replied, hesitated, then turned and followed the others, trying to cover her breasts with a torn bodice.

Is there a good way to die? Chatham silently asked the body. He left the prison without waiting for the answer.

He caught up with the others on the veranda, the dull ache in his belly spreading and almost causing him to hunch over. Dampierre had cut the sixth nun free from the stake and now she lay over his arms, twitching occasionally in semiconsciousness.

"Make for the north," Chatham ordered while scanning the opposite direction. The choppers were still firing at the unseen tribesmen. Dampierre led off at a trot, carrying the body as if it were weightless. L'Escaut and Gertewoute forced the five nuns along, helping them to their feet when they stumbled. Rochereau and Chatham brought up the rear, pausing often to fire at the growing number of pursuers. Chatham gritted his teeth at each jolting recoil of the machine pistol.

Rochereau fired at two blacks as they ran the gap between two huts. The bullets kicked up a cloud of dust from the mud walls. The dead warriors' momentum hurled them through the dust, causing them to appear suddenly—like magician's assistants. There was no applause and the dead lay where they fell. Arrows began to fall around the rear guard. Chatham's leaden legs stumbled, and his lungs labored to keep the fires stoked with oxygen. Chatham couldn't tell whether it was due to blood loss or if poison was already working its way through his system.

A grunt came from Rochereau. Chatham saw him fall with a poisoned arrow shaft sticking out of his throat. Chatham shouted his name and plucked a fragmentation grenade from his shoulder harness. The Frenchman caught the tossed frag clumsily in both hands and rolled heavily into the dirt *John Wayne would have shouldered him and heroically cut his way to freedom;* Chatham thought, *but I'm sure as hell not like the Duke was and this wasn't The Sands of Iwo Jima.* He lost sight of the downed Frenchman as he turned and followed the others. He heard a collective howl as the pursuers caught sight of the fallen man.

The struggling band of whites broke out of the village. Ten seconds later, the dull crump of the exploding grenade thudded in the humid air, and more than one scream echoed the explosion. Rochereau took a few with him. Those few didn't make that much difference to the living, but maybe it made his last moments a little better.

Through the thinning mist, a fourth helicopter rocketed over the treetops from the north. It slewed around as it settled heavily into the grass. Its landing gear bounced on the turf once, then remained hovering about a foot off the ground. The soldiers pitched the women up to the waiting crew chief. Chatham lobbed two grenades beyond the outer line of huts as the rest scrambled aboard. The grenades exploded, then Chatham tossed the machine pistol inside and leaped for the door. He landed on the edge of the hatch, tendrils of pain eating into his brain. His legs still dangled outside when the pilot applied full throttle. The chopper shot upward like a released balloon. He was hauled in by several strong hands and was unceremoniously flopped on the deck. A few arrows followed as over fifty warriors surged into the vacated clearing.

The chopper gained a safe altitude and Chatham's men joined the doorgunner in pouring full auto fire onto the dancing figures below. The ground fog had been burnt away by the sun, and they could see the Mpeche streaming through the village. The firing stopped only when all the ammo was gone.

The three diversionary helicopters joined in formation, leaving the unsprung trap behind. The crew chief unlimbered a first aid kit and began ministering to the women, some of whom were sobbing uncontrollably.

The four men slumped against the fuselage. The copilot passed out cigarettes to the weary, silent figures and lit them. Chatham caught the sergeant major's eye and motioned him over. When the older man saw the shirtfront, he retrieved another medic kit and went to work, his pinched face carefully expressionless. He had to cut the web belt, the blow of the spearhead having smashed and forced the buckle halves together. The Saviors of Zamboji Mission were going home for a rest. Hallelujah, the Lord was on their side.

CHAPTER TWO

Soldiering, my dear madam, is the coward's art of attacking mercilessly when you are strong, and keeping out of harm's way when you are weak.

G. B. Shaw, *Arms and the Man*

The sun was well up and the Colonel could hear muffled sounds from the busy orderly room. He moved to the sandbagged window overlooking the dusty parade ground and lit another cigarette. He shifted his glance to the contour map covering one wall. *The raid should be underway by now.*

The commander wished that he had had time to keep Chatham out of this one, now that the break had finally come. After so much waiting, it would be ironic if Chatham was killed in the skirmish. Luckily, stoicism didn't breed ulcers.

The Colonel was frankly surprised at himself at being a natural player in the game of deception. In past battles, loyalties and opponents had been clearly defined and he could devote his full attention to strategy. But he found that serving several masters added just a few more facets to an already complicated vocation.

And Chatham, there was another natural. Try as he might, the Colonel had detected nothing out of character in the younger man. He was a player with no past and future when offstage. The Colonel had the feeling that Chatham had been a player far longer than himself.

Now the bait had been taken and the game would get hotter. The point was approaching where there could be no turning back. Chatham would begin his performance in earnest and the Colonel would wait in the wings. Wait, to begin a supporting role or claim the body. Provided, of course, that Chatham wasn't disposed of in the dressing room.

The Colonel flipped the cigarette butt out of the window, cleared his mind and returned to the paper work on his desk.

Sabre One. Home wasn't particularly sweet, but it was secure. Headquarters of the 3rd Paracommando Regiment was a fort built to withstand any forseeable guerrilla attack: a triangle with packed earth, log, and sandbagged walls rising six feet. At each corner was a circular mortar pit and heavy machine gun post, with machine gun bunkers placed at intervals along the walls. In the center of the base stood a reinforced fire control tower. Directly outside and imbedded in the wall itself, were sharpened punji stakes. To get to the twenty-five-meter-wide ring of stakes, attackers had to wade through a barrier of tangle foot barbed wire. And fifty meters beyond this, were triple strands of concertina wire. Sabre I had been built on the edge of the jungle in the foothills of the rising plateau. The thin forest had been cut back one eighth of a mile from the fort, the felled trees being used in the walls. Their absence provided a barren fire zone buffer. A Viet Cong sapper would penetrate the defenses in two minutes. But the local amateurs could be held at bay indefinitely. Until they got tanks and mortars and learned how to use them, they were no threat.

Luxury is a comparative thing. Basic necessities for an insurance salesman in Manhattan were luxuries in this hunting ground. The security of Sabre I allowed Chatham eighteen hours of unguarded sleep. When he awoke, he spent thirty minutes gingerly scrubbing grime and camouflage paint from his body. The shower water was unheated, coming from the roof storage tank. But it was clean and vermin free. When the flight from Zamboji dropped him off at the pad, the medics took him to an overworked medical officer. The m.o. briskly pronounced the superficial belly wound free of poison and closed it neatly with five stitches. Chatham dressed in a clean tiger suit and jungle boots, buckled on a pistol belt, put on his red para beret and walked through the cool morning to the mess hall. Even though it was his first hot meal in a week, he routinely ate a light breakfast. He did indulge in several glasses of iced tea. No one had asked where the ice making machine had come from. But it was well guarded to make sure that it did not return to its previous owner.

He then returned leisurely to the officers' barracks. Like most of Sabre I's buildings, it was a single-story wooden longhouse surrounded by a four-foot-high, anti-blast, sandbag wall. He reached the front door just as the Officer of the Day rounded the corner. Lieutenant Framere saluted, then stretched out his hand.

"I'm glad to see you back, Erik."

"It's good to be back, David."

"How long will you be here this time?"

"Like usual, I guess. I have a debriefing with Regimental Intelligence. One of my men bought the farm and I need a replacement. Sergeant major's out headhunting now. Suppose I'll be back with First Battalion in two or three days." He took a pack of cigarettes from his fatigues. When they had both fired up, he continued, "What about you, David? When do you get your release and another chance to get your balls cut off?"

Framere laughed. He thought it sounded like George Peppard. "They say the leg is healed. But they have to find a new slot for me before I can get back out. Out into it, I mean."

"I don't envy you, pulling duty here. Looks like you just spent a tour of OD. Could use some sleep, I suppose?" Chatham never felt quite at ease with Framere. Besides, his reserve of small talk never had been overly abundant.

"For sure, Erik. I have one message to deliver,

then I'm off duty. You are to report to the Old Man in the bunker as soon as possible."

"Know what it's about?"

"Maybe he wants a debriefing on the rescue operation."

"No, he'll get that from Intelligence." Chatham ground his cigarette butt in the dust. "Well, I'll soon find out. Get some rest, David."

"See you later, Captain."

The sun dampened the back and armpits of Chatham's fresh shirt on the way to the command bunker. The base was stirring to life and the third relief perimeter guards were on their way to the mess hall before turning in.

The command bunker lay at the foot of the fire control tower and next to the headquarters building. Two red bereted guards stood in a MG emplacement at the entrance. No bearskins or chromed bayonets, but the MAG machine gun was spotless and the British style salutes snappy. This wasn't true in some merc units. Chatham was glad to see it. To ex-legionaires, strict discipline was a security blanket. Chatham's return salute was palm down, U.S.A. issue. Old habits were hard to break. He stepped into the darkened entrance.

The bunker was one large room half underground and completely encased in sandbags. It offered more privacy than the HQ itself. Light filtering through the firing slits was aided by several bare bulbs. Maps with esoteric symbols covered the walls. Desks and tables held field phones and wireless sets. Against the far wall, seated at a large desk, was Colonel Theodore Wilhelm von Heydeck.

The deeply tanned commander of the 3rd Regiment was lean and fit for a man in his fifties. Light blond hair topping a seamed and weathered face was shot with gray. The golden crown and crossed sabres of his rank badges sparkled on the epaulets of his tiger suit, as did the winged dagger beret badge on the desk in front of him. There were no decorations on his battle dress even though he had fought his way from Smolensk to Moscow, Hanoi to Saigon, Algiers to Oran and Katanga to Leopoldville. A brilliant officer, politics had suckered him onto the losing side in all of his wars. He had learned a lot as panzer leader and Foreign Legion para. His company dossier had been quite detailed. Those who enter the Foreign Legion to forget aren't necessarily forgotten.

His viking blue eyes looked up from the papers on his desk, and he got to his feet. "Come in, Captain. Please be at ease." His British accent didn't match his past.

The younger soldier saluted, swept off his cover and holstered M-59 and deposited them both on a table, still within reach. Chatham perched on the edge and folded his arms.

"You wished to see me, Colonel?"

"Yes." He sat down and squared the papers before him. "First, let me congratulate you on your mission. I am pleased that your wound was minor. The Generalissimo seems pleased with the results."

"Yes, I expected he would be. I understand the women were transferred to a plane when we got in. Should be in a hospital in Lamapur by now."

"No doubt battling the reporters as they did the blacks." It was a flat statement, unsoftened by a smile. "I see you lost a man."

"Yes. One experienced trooper for six nuns. Someone farther removed should tally the score, I suppose."

"A point taken differently in different circles."

"It was a waste. Those damned missionaries put themselves in the cannibal pot and they could damn well crawl out by themselves."

"Some people would not be at all pleased to hear those words."

Chatham smiled. "I don't say them around some people."

"I am sure I will receive a full report from Intelligence this afternoon," the Colonel said, dismissing the subject. "The reason that I asked you here was to inform you of your new assignment."

Reassignment wasn't unexpected. Being one of the few merc officers who had bothered to learn the local dialect, Chatham was continually being shuffled between battalions fulfilling his intelligence duties.

"To whom should I report this time?"

Colonel von Heydeck picked up a sheet of paper. "Your orders state that you should report to the commanding officer of the Household Guards at the Imperial High Command—God, they are fond of titles—in Lamapur no later than twenty-four hundred hours from now."

Chatham's neutral expression masked his pleasure. The Colonel handed him several copies of the orders. He read them through in silence, then, in case there was an unseen audience, he began his act.

"Sir, it is nearly impossible for me to abandon my present duties. You, surely, will admit that you need me. Who will take over my squad?"

"I have assigned Lieutenant Framere to take your squad. He is fully recovered from his wounds and is quite ready for reassignment."

"Framere! He may be ready physically but otherwise I doubt if he ever will be." Chatham was laying it on pretty thick, but he thought it would pass as natural concern for his men. "There is still a question as to whether it was his negligence that lost half of his old platoon. I don't want him killing my squad too." Righteous indignation wasn't his forte. But, then, there wasn't an overabundance of drama critics in the 3rd.

"That is enough, Captain. There is no choice. We are spread thin now. Your orders seem to originate at high government levels. If there were any other way, I assure you, you would not be leaving now."

Chatham restudied the orders. "They don't state the reason for the transfer. Are there any other par-as stationed in the capital?"

"The Second Battalion of the Second protects important installations in and around Lamapur. But if you were seconded to them, the orders would say so. I have not been informed of the reason. I can only trust that the Field Marshal, in his infinite wisdom, has greater need of you than I. I've got a

Saladin laid on for you. It will leave HZ at thirteen hundred hours. That should get you to the depot in time to catch the train. Draw what you need from the quartermaster."

Chatham buckled on his pistol belt and turned toward the entrance.

"Oh yes, one more thing," von Heydeck said quietly. The German held out more printed papers in his left hand and two epaulet sleeves in his right. "I have also received your promotion orders."

Chatham didn't have to fake puzzlement as he put on his beret. Service in this outfit was not marked by speedy promotion.

"The orders are effective as of yesterday," von Heydeck continued, "so you might as well put these on before you leave."

Chatham accepted the insignia, glanced down at them and looked back at von Heydeck. "Lieutenant Colonel?"

"It seems our Generalissimo has seen fit to jump the rank of major entirely."

"Mother always said I'd go far in my chosen profession."

"Indeed."

"Goodbye, Colonel. I'll be back as soon as this is cleared up."

"Good-bye, Lieutenant Colonel." They exchanged salutes. Chatham heard von Heydeck's last word, muttered in German. "Politics," he said.

Along with the other two, Chatham smoked in the shade of the deserted depot. The afternoon heat made the cigarette stick to his sweaty fingers and taste bitter in his dry throat.

The two officers sat in the dust, leaning against the rough cinderblock wall while the trooper perched on the turret of the Saladin armored car. Even at ease, professionals never move far from their protection or weapons.

The five-mile trip from Sabre I was peaceful, probably due to the menacing armament of the light armored vehicle. The dirt road, almost nonexistent in some places, ran through the jungle for most of its length and sniping archers had been known to skewer the unwary. Even with the hatches open, the interior of the car had been hot and cramped. The quarters were so close that the gunner/radioman had been left behind to make room for Chatham. Because of the heat, he and Lt. Becker had stood in the turret hatches. Arrows they could dodge, heat they couldn't.

The scant cooling breeze created by motion disappeared when they halted at the destination. They knew by experience that they couldn't escape the wet heat even by remaining still, so they ignored it. The empty depot, even with the missing doors and windows, was cooler than the shade outside. In times of normalcy, the single building beside the narrow-gage track would have been crowded with chattering natives waiting to take produce to the city market. The stationmaster had been decapitated in front of the ticket office by the rebels and, since then, the building had been deserted.

* * *

Small talk passed the time. Recent massacres and retaliatory strikes instead of golf scores and commuter trains.

The driver, Giraud, ended the conversation by flipping away his cigarette butt and swinging his feet down onto the engine compartment. Chatham stiffened and reached for his machine pistol.

"The train is coming, sir."

Becker and Chatham relaxed, then got to their feet. Faintly, the sound of the steam engine reached them before the train itself broke out of the jungle about one hundred meters down the track. The ancient black engine gave the impression of laboring up a nonexistent steep incline. The cowcatcher was rusty, the smokestack sooty, and the layers of dust were uniform. The train was not long. Behind the engine and wood car came a flatcar ringed by a three-foot-high wall of sandbags. Along with about twenty-five Zakariyan riflemen were several light machine guns. A vintage passenger coach and two decrepit freight cars with guards atop brought up the rear.

The engine shuddered to a halt amid much hissing and screeching. "Give a country to the damn wogs and see what happens," Lt. Becker observed disgustedly.

As the train stopped, a Zakariyan major swung down from the armored cab and strutted towards them. His tan dress uniform, complete with Sam Browne belt and bogus battle ribbons, would have been resplendent except for one thing. The major's sweat had reduced the military creases to a mass of wrinkles. Dark stains crept from under the arms and the shirt collar, and his khaki tie had wilted into a limp ribbon.

On each hip, he carried a four-inch barreled revolver with ivory grips. All well and good if an officer with a Patton complex, Lord protect us, spent all of his time on parade in Lamapur, thought Chatham, but they are a bad choice for a working man. The revolvers were more apt to fail to function, harder to clean, less accurate, and lacked the fire power of the self-loaders carried by most of the mercs.

The small, moustached officer halted in front of Chatham and smartly touched the brim of his garrison cap with the tip of his swagger stick.

"My orders are to halt this train to pick up a passenger." The major made a poor attempt at an Etonian accent. "I take that passenger to be yourself, Colonel?" His tone implied that it would take at least a colonel to stop the train.

"That's correct, Major. . .?"

"Major Mahadi, at your service." The sarcastic smile and stiff bow made the offer a lie. "If you would be so good as to board immediately, we will arrive all the sooner in the capital."

Lt. Becker, ignored until now, said, "Major, would you please have one of your men load the Colonel's baggage? We also wish to speed you on your way."

Mahadi turned slowly, arrogantly to face the merc. "My detachment, Lieutenant, is assigned to provide security for this train and nothing else. They are not beasts of burden."

"Would you consider it a breach of military etiquette, Major, to require the Colonel to carry his own baggage?" Lt. Becker's voice was deceptively calm.

"Perhaps you would be so good as to carry the Colonel's personal belongings yourself?" the Major said with an insolent sneer.

Becker's tanned face grew ruddier. "Major, I wouldn't allow one of my orderlies to take over for one of your rear echelon desk generals!"

"Watch your step, Lieutenant! I have powerful friends!" Mahadi barked.

"Of course. How else would you have risen to your present rank?"

The Major's voice quivered and his knuckles whitened on his swagger stick. "Tread very, very carefully, Lieutenant! I have twenty-five marksmen at my orders!"

"I suppose that makes us about even then, Major. You may have noticed my driver entering the turret of my Saladin. The cannon is loaded with cannister shot. If you are not familiar with the round, perhaps you will allow me to enlighten you? It holds eight hundred steel pellets, designed for use against massed infantry at short ranges. My driver is a highly qualified gunner."

There was silence as Mahadi peered past them to the eyes of Giraud through the gunner's hatch on the turret. The long barrel was directed at the flatcar where the riflemen chattered and smoked, unaware. The 76-mm gun would cut them to shreds like an over-sized alloy gun.

"My bags are against the wall, Major," Chatham said, ending the tense silence.

Mahadi yelled over his shoulder, "Sergeant! Two men for the Colonel's bags! Immediately!"

Chatham turned to Becker and shook his hand. "Good hunting." Becker nodded as Chatham slung the machine pistol on his back. He strolled to the passenger coach and the native grunts deposited his duffels on the entrance platform beside him. Mahadi remounted the engine and, after the soldiers scrambled onto the flatcar, the train slowly got under way. Chatham watched until the depot was out of his line of sight.

"Wogs certainly like to palaver, don't you think?"

He turned and faced the man standing in the doorframe. Tall and slim, it was difficult to tell his age. His narrow wrinkled face topped by sandy hair could have been that of a man from twenty-five to forty. His large, toothy smile gave the stranger an innocent, boyish air. Chatham guessed him to be British, both by his accent and his immaculate tropical whites. Britishers seem to do their best to deny the existence of sweat glands—and usually succeed.

"Please do come in out of the sun. Heaven knows, the coach is anything but cool, but at least one can rest one's feet." Chatham followed to the interior of the empty, brokendown coach.

The Englishman sank gracefully into a cracked leather seat. Chatham sat in one facing him and fished in his breast pocket for a crumpled pack of cigarettes. A silver, crested cigarette case appeared in the Englishman's manicured fingers.

"Do have one of mine—'specially made, you know. One of my indulgences." The face split into a sheepish grin, apologetically. Chatham accepted one and tried to think where you could find a manicurist in Ma'ribassa.

"Thank you, Mr. . .?"

"Oh yes, how absentminded of me! Baden-Balfour's the name. Frederick Basil Baden-Balfour, actually. Dreadfully long and unwieldy, I'm afraid, so call me Freddy. Everyone else does." Even wandering ju ju men? Chatham wondered. Freddy lit Chatham's cigarette, then his own with a matching silver lighter.

"Erik Chatham."

"So pleased to meet you, Colonel. I so rarely get the opportunity to meet you Gentlemen Soldiers, ha ha, being tied up in Lamapur, and all."

"What are you tied to?"

"Tied to? Oh yes! I say, very good! What am I tied to. Yes, well, I'm with the embassy, actually. Nothing outstanding, really. Undersecretary of Economics. Out here on business, you see. Looking over a lumber mill site. Seems Her Majesty may want to assist somewhat, as soon as the troubles end. In consequence, I had to leave my air conditioner and walk about in the bush, so to speak. Weather's beastly. For a white man, anyway. How do you chaps stand it?"

Chatham smiled and said, "Willpower."

Freddy winked. "Those stacks of money in the numbered accounts, what?"

"I thought mad dogs and Englishmen . . ."

"Oh dear, for some, maybe. I doubt if I ever would have left London if Father hadn't thought it would be good for me. Public service, House of Lords, and all. But no piker is Freddy! If this be my lot among the heathen, then I'll do my best and pray for a transfer! But, here I am, blithering on about me. I must keep a close eye on my manners. What moves you to be on the Capital Express?"

"I've received a transfer. I'm to report for new duty in Lamapur. Perhaps I could visit your air conditioner."

"Oh yes! Be my pleasure, actually!" Freddy leaned forward and whispered, "I do have some intimate knowledge of certain night spots, where, for a small fee . . ."

"I don't doubt it, Freddy. Maybe we could talk about it over a beer sometime. Right now, I'd like to catch up on some sleep while I can."

"They all say that, then I never see them again," Freddy griped petulantly as he made room for Chatham's boots. Chatham smiled good-naturedly and eased himself deeper into the complaining seat.

In thirty minutes, Chatham was jolted from his nap and seat and wound up amid the garbage on the floor. After the initial violent jerk, the train slowed almost to a standstill. Freddy peered dazedly over the back rest of his seat.

Chatham scrambled to his feet, retrieved his machine pistol and headed toward the front of the train.

"I say! What's happened?" Freddy's question went unanswered as Chatham slipped through the door.

The troopers on the flatcar were still in jumbled confusion. He shouldered his way through them to the wood car. As he slipped down the loose cord wood, he saw the fireman in a corner of the cab watching Mahadi whip a cowering black engineer with his swagger stick. He took it away from the major and tossed it out a window. Mahadi swung to face him, his face livid.

Chatham's sharp tone halted him. "That won't help what's happened. By the way, what has happened?"

"There was a man on the track!" Mahadi began, his voice high with tension. "I told this idiot to keep going and run him over! But the superstitious ass wouldn't because he was a ju ju man! Now we are stopped here because of one ignorant savage on the tracks!"

"Not exactly correct. Looks like he brought some friends to the party." The native officer followed Chatham's gaze through the cab's front viewing port.

From the jungle on both sides, black warriors were emerging by the dozen, crowding across the tracks. Chatham couldn't make out what the witchman was saying, but it was having its effect on the growing band. Spears and *semes* flashed in outstretched fists, and angry shouts lifted above the noise of the halted engine.

Mhadi stared at the crowd of about one hundred painted Mpeche. He broke out of his trance and began to scramble up the wood pile. Chatham grabbed his collar and dragged him back into the cab. He was aware that Freddy had joined them.

"Where are you going, Major?"

"To order my men to fire! Cut the rebels down before they cut our throats!"

"Too many for that."

"And what would you do, mighty mercenary?"

"I thought we'd go and have a talk with them."

Mahadi's eyes widened. "You don't expect me to go down *there?*"

Chatham sighed. "No, I suppose not. Now please listen carefully, Major. If any one of your men fires, I will personally blow your brains out, if some Mpeche doesn't beat me to it. If, on the other hand, I open up, please feel free to join in on the chorus."

He let go of the little man, shrugged the machine pistol into position and started to swing down from the cab. Freddy crowded in behind him.

"Where are you going, as if I had to ask?"

"Good heavens, I'd like to see the blighters close up. Make a great story at Dad's club!"

"One place is as safe an another, I suppose. Stay close behind me and don't do anything without consulting me first. Except breathe occasionally, if you can work it in."

He stepped to the ground and was immediately surrounded by sweating, jostling Mpeche. He slowly and firmly shouldered his way to the front of the engine where the witchman was reading the riot act.

A small space opened in front of the leader and

Chatham looked him over as he approached. The ju ju man was small and very old, dressed in a ragged pair of shorts and sandals. Bandoliers festooned his skinny chest, hung with dried gourds, small animal skins and teeth, and other unrecognizable odds and ends.

A large black with rotten teeth, bloodshot eyes, and stripes of paint streaking face and chest, waved a *seme* sword menacingly in Chatham's direction. "Now Hamuraba will show the power! All the whites will die! Guns will not stop us!"

Chatham lifted his voice, answering in their dialect, "This is indeed wondrous. Hamuraba's power must be strong. Even I, Mloku-arambi-chlapaku, have heard of it." If anything would slow the pace down, it would be the opportunity to make a speech.

"That it is, Smiler!" the big black turned to face his brethren. "Did he not show to us the miracle two days past?" The answering roar confirmed. "Did not his own son fire the rifle at his chest, and did he not but laugh and wipe the water away?" Again the mob howled.

Hamuraba remained silent throughout, sneering across the three feet that separated him from the white man. Chatham gazed back, then turned to face the mob.

"I would speak with the mighty Hamuraba and learn more of this miracle, for I too wish to see and believe." Another roar crashed around his ears.

Chatham stepped in close to the ju ju man and leaned close to his wrinkled face. His body shielded the machine pistol from the view of the war band as Chatham shoved the barrel into the little black's belly.

Chatham spoke English in a low, conversational tone. "I'm not your son, old shit, and this gun is not loaded with blanks. If I pull the trigger, it will cut you in half."

A high squeaky voice piped out of the skinny throat, answering in English. "The others will rip you apart in your tracks!"

"Not before I spit in your blood. You have lived far too long, but your life still is a thing of value to you, isn't it, lizard? There is only one way for you to walk away still holding that miserable life cupped in your hands. The train will move. We will be sitting on the front, you and I. When we are past the warriors, I will allow you to leave unharmed."

"They will never allow it. I can no longer stop them." Hamuraba's face was like stone.

"Then you must speak to them. If they listen, you will make love to more diseased crocodiles before your overdue death."

The old man hesitated and Chatham pushed the barrel in a little deeper. When he next spoke, it was again in dialect:

"I have read the omens! This is not the time to show our true strength! The enemies are few and only the cowardly Arabs! Their hearts will give us no nourishment! We will let these dogs go and they will send many red hats to us and we will bathe in their blood!"

After a pause, the frowns turned to laughter and the blacks roared.

"This white snake has begged me to ride with him on the iron cart to honor me! I will instruct him in the message to carry to the dog-shit Arabs!"

Between the cheers, Chatham spoke over his shoulder, "Freddy, you still there?"

"Right behind you, mate."

"Go back to Mahadi. Tell him to move the train out slow until we get beyond the tribesmen, then open up the throttle. And tell him again—no firing or we die."

"Righto, mate. I'm on my way."

"Time for us to board, grandfather. Climb the cowcatcher slow and sit on the far side."

The old man was agile, but climbed cautiously. Chatham followed when he was seated on the iron frame. Hamuraba stared straight ahead with feigned dignity. Chatham smiled brightly but kept the machine pistol wedged in the old man's side.

The train began to move forward and the cheering Mpeche melted off the track. The beat of the pistons accelerated as the train steadily picked up speed. The pair sat in silence for several minutes.

"I shall dismount now," the ju ju man said bitterly.

"And so you shall, grandfather. For, you see, we soldiers are practical men." Chatham smiled.

Hamuraba rose to climb down the side of the cowcatcher. Chatham placed his hand in the middle of the bony back and shoved straight forward. Catlike, the ju ju twisted in mid-air and sprawled heavily in the gravel inches from the steel wheels. He disappeared from sight before Chatham could move.

"Should have shot the bastard in the first place," he muttered, disgusted with himself.

He reslung his weapon, climbed back along the engine catwalk and swung into the cab. Mahadi stood in the corner, aloof from the busy crewmen and grinning Englishman.

"Everything in control, I see, Major. Well, keep up the good work and you might get a mention in dispatches. Come on, Freddy. I still need my rest."

The two men returned to the coach and Freddy produced more cigarettes.

"Freddy, have you ever been in the army?"

"Good heavens, yes! How did you know? Royal Catering Corps. 'They also serve, etc.' Father said that some military service was better than none, don't you know. For the record, House of Lords and all."

"Quite."

"I say, that was all very splendid, old boy. But one thing bothers me a bit."

"What's that, Freddy?"

"Well, surely you took a terrible risk. What if the witch doctor had been like the rest of those savages and hadn't understood English? How could you have threatened him without the others knowing?"

"He wore sandals."

"Beg pardon?"

"Bush Mpeche never wear shoes. They've got callouses on their feet a quarter of an inch thick. That meant the ju ju man was a city Mpeche, which in turn means that he has to know a little English, if simply to take orders."

"I say! Elementary, what! Quite thrilling! Wait until I write home!"

Chatham settled himself in his seat and blocked out the sun by pulling his beret over his face.

CHAPTER THREE

Now what are the two things that happen to a soldier so often that he comes to think nothing of them? One is hearing people tell lies; the other is getting his life saved in all sorts of ways by all sorts of people.

G. B. Shaw, *Arms and the Man*

Ma'ribassa's palace intrigues were a can of worms, but geographically, it was a simple country. A small African nation, it was attacked from the west by man-eating jungle and from the east by the Indian Ocean. The jungle and its children, swamp and disease, had barred even black migration. Along the edge of the sea, coastal swamps had kept out Western and Eastern imperialists alike. And these coastal waters had shallow mud flats that discouraged all vessels but canoe and raft. The invasion of first the Arab rulers, and later the European, were made overland from the north, following the route of the Kasambi River. When the river split, one branch cascading into the sunken jungle bowl and the other passing through the eastern plateau to the sea, the invaders wisely chose to follow the latter. After scattering the conquered Mpeche into the inhospitable jungle, the Arabs built their cities and seated their power on the plateau. They entered the jungle only to steal its wealth and tribesmen. Much later, when they were able, they gutted the Eastern Kasambi with dredges to create a shipping lifeline running from Lamapur to the sea.

The train made slow progress up the Great Escarpment because of the uncountable switchbacks. Each turn sloughed off more of the jungle humidity and stench. When the top of the plateau was finally reached, the stiff, cool wind blowing inland seemed almost arid. From there, the rails ran straight through the rolling grasslands and allowed the train to put on speed. It arrived in the capital shortly before dusk.

Freddy offered to share a taxi as they dismounted at the central station, but the offer was unnecessary. A Zakariyan NCO met Chatham at the loading platform and escorted him to a waiting staff car. He said goodbye to Freddy while the driver loaded his baggage, then climbed in the limousine. The driver seemed to know where he was headed, so Chatham sat back and relaxed in the air-conditioned silence. He tried to make some sense, for about the tenth time, out of the developments.

He wasn't displeased. His goal had been to get assigned to the capital. But the assignment had come ass backward. After spending some time doing the job he had been hired for, raising a smoke screen, von Heydeck was supposed to use some pretext to get him into Lamapur. But the opposition had beat the conspirators to the trigger and seemingly played into their hands. Chatham always mistrusted windfalls on principle. Occupational disease. You must admit, it doesn't seem quite kosher when the man that you are supposed to assassinate orders you to breathe down his neck.

The odds were slim that Tashfin had completely burned his cover. If he cared to check, he could easily find out that Chatham was an ex-Special Forces officer cashiered because of some CIA-inspired dirty tricks. Which, of course, he wasn't. Somewhere, in a little corner of a building in Virginia, resided his 201 file intact. He got promotions and bennies like any line officer. And provided he stayed alive long enough, someday he would probably reappear in army green. Detached duty to the Company, although very secretive, is also very lucrative. A lot of brass in the Pentagon answer hurriedly when "40" calls, "40" being the secret committee of advisors to DCI, the Director of Central Intelligence.

It was also possible that the Field Marshal had somehow learned of his training at the Farm and his membership in the Kill Team. But if that were the case, he would, at the very least, make sure that Chatham remained in the boonies hassling with the enemies of the state. And more likely, he would have Chatham "terminated with extreme prejudice."

Chatham had always been amused by the efforts

of the top dogs to sanitize the dirty realities. If you blow a mark's head off with a long gun or knot a piano wire around his neck, you are "terminating with extreme prejudice." If you need information badly and, in the course of the questioning, things get messy, you are administering a "strong interrogation." If an agent is burned and thrown to the wolves by denying his existence, he is "zeroed." And Chatham's line of work is called "special." World War II had the Office of Special Services, Special Operations Executive, and Special Air Service. The Company has its Special Operations Group and Special Operations Division. The political game is easier to play when the politicos aren't forced to stick their noses in their own shit.

It was too soon for Chatham to decide his next move. He needed more info before he could decide whether to abort or take countermeasures. He wouldn't have been in this position if it was to be a simple hit. If that were the case, he could be infiltrated in any number of ways, waste Tashfin with a scoped rifle or silenced pistol and be exfiltrated, all inside of a week.

If war is just an extension of politics, then assassination is even more so. It was useless to ask Chatham why the Company wanted Tashfin out of the way. The gun is rarely informed of why the trigger is pulled. Maybe the fate of the free world rested in his hands, but he strongly doubted it. More like increased export of bananas to the U.S.

He wasn't completely in the dark, but his need to know was limited. *Fact:* He had to kill Tashfin as

soon as possible and still accomplish the goal. *Fact:*
The hit had to be coordinated with von Heydeck so
that he could occupy the capital with the 3rd and
hand over power to Kumi, the opposition leader.
Do all this and still get out alive. The last condition
was at the top of Chatham's list of priorities. It
probably wasn't given much consideration by anyone else.

It goes without saying, if anything went wrong,
von Heydeck and Chatham would be zeroed. A
plausible denial would be easy. But that didn't
weigh heavily on his mind. If anything did go
wrong, he would be dead long before diplomatic
channels heated up.

The limo had left the slums behind. The streets
were still narrow, but the buildings were not de-
caying hulks and the crush of people had lessened.
The pedestrians were of the middle class, at least by
Ma'ribassan standards.

Like a slide lecture, the scene abruptly changed
again. Vehicular traffic increased on the wide
boulevards, clean and framed by greenery. The
buildings were mostly stores or government offices.
It was Tashfin's showcase, maintained at great expense to impress influential visitors.

The driver pulled into one of the many plazas
dotting the city. A large mounted statue of the cur-
rent emperor, Irgun Isam-al-Khamlanadur, domi-
nated the square from its center. Taking up one side
was a many-storied, balconied building labeled the
Hotel International. The obvious elegance was only

minimally marred by the sandbagged guardpost manned at the entrance by paras.

Chatham picked up the intercom mike and spoke to the driver on the other side of the glass partition.

"What's that building we just passed?"

"Hotel International, sir. One of our finest. The guests are mostly foreigners, journalists, high officials and the like. I'm told it is very pleasant, sir."

That explained the paras. To make sure the right people weren't inconsiderate enough to get wasted by the rebels. The hotel could be considered an important government installation.

"Where else are units of the second on duty?"

The driver answered without hesitation. He had obviously been instructed to provide Chatham with anything he required.

"Units are assigned to government buildings in the city and, of course, the Imperial Palace. Also, within the city, the radio station, waterworks, and electrical station are guarded. The only unit outside the city is on the coast at the river mouth to protect incoming ships. Of course, many other locations are guarded by Imperial troops."

Chatham cradled the mike. It was easy to gauge the importance of any installation by checking on which unit was assigned to guard it. Imperial troops were notorious for deserting their posts at the exhaust backfire of a truck.

About ten minutes after leaving the square, they pulled up to the courtyard gates of a large, gray stone building flying the Ma'ribassan flag. The high Command was located in the local version of the Pentagon. Quite a bit smaller, but with the same percentage of uniformed bureaucrats. Chatham's papers were checked by the guard, then the limo passed through to the spacious courtyard and pulled up to the main entrance. Chatham was standing on the steps casing the place before the driver could reach his door.

In a tone implying that things like that just weren't done, he said, "If you will report to the front desk, sir, you will be given directions to the commandant's office. I will stay with your luggage here." He motioned in the direction of other parked limos. "At your pleasure, sir."

Chatham tossed his machine pistol on the back seat and mounted the steps. He returned the salutes at the colonnaded entrance and entered the cool, dark interior. He paused while his eyes adjusted to the dimness.

Brass scurried about a large reception desk, heels clacking on marble, anxiously clutching papers to bemedaled chests. Chatham approached the CSM at the desk. He looked up with the disdain of an enlisted man daily wielding power over officers.

"Yes sir?" He wasn't about to waste words on a connectionless mercenary light colonel.

"Colonel Chatham to see the commandant of the Metro Military District."

He made a show of searching through the papers on his desk, then picked up a sheet that had been on the top throughout. He read from the sheet, then pulled a plastic ident card from a drawer and tossed it across the desk.

"Pin that on, please, sir. Then if you will hand over your side arm to me," he said as he glanced at Chatham's holstered 9-mm, "I will have an orderly conduct you to Commandant Khalifa's office."

"I hate to be a bother, Sergeant. Just give me the room number and I will find my own way. *With* my side arm."

A wary look passed over the officer's face. His hand moved to the edge of the desk and dropped softly to his lap.

Chatham placed both hands on the center of the desk top and leaned over until he was about twelve inches from the NCO's face. "If you're playing with your cock, I won't bother you. If you're holding anything else, I'll take your arm off at the elbow."

The young man hesitated, reviewing the consequences of his next move. If he tried to shoot and wasn't fast enough, he had Chatham to worry about. If he was fast enough, he had the commandant to worry about, at the very least. He replaced his hand on the desk. Before picking up the ident card, Chatham crushed the papers under his balled fists and let them flutter back down to the desk. He pinned the badge on, watching the silent NCO.

"The room?"

"Room five-eighteen." His eyes slid to the floor. "The elevator is to your right." Chatham remained where he was. ". . . sir," he added quietly. Chatham didn't move until the sergeant reluctantly snapped a salute. Then he smiled and walked to the waiting elevator.

The operator left him off on the fifth floor and he easily found the office he was looking for. He was ushered through the reception room and admitted to the commandant's room immediately.

Commandant Khalifa was a pleasant surprise. Instead of an overweight, overdecorated desk pusher, Chatham found an intense, fit, and relatively young full colonel. There was only a single row of ribbons on his chest, but all were awarded for valor in combat. A post responsible for the security of the Generalissimo would not be sold to the highest bidder.

Khalifa came around his desk and greeted Chatham with reserve. If he wasn't overjoyed to see the interloper, neither was he antagonistic. Chatham was settled in a chair, accepted a cigarette, refused the hard stuff and opted for lemonade. Pleasantries duly exchanged, Colonel Khalifa got to the point.

"Your orders do not state the reason for your reassignment, and I have no doubt that you would like to resolve the mystery."

"Correct, Colonel. I have been going through possibilities during my journey, but rejected them all. I can't come up with any plausible excuse for the transfer."

"Frankly, neither can I, Colonel Chatham."

"Pardon?"

Khalifa sighed. "Like you, I have not been informed as to what your duties shall be. I do know why you were ordered to report to me, however. It was to amend the orders as follows." Khalifa picked up a sheet of expensive stationary. "Colonel

A. Khalifa, Commandant, etc., etc. My dear Ali: You will have by now received your copy of orders issued by this headquarters assigning Colonel E. Chatham, First Battalion, Third Regiment, Volunteer Territorial Paracommandos, to your headquarters. He is to report to you personally by nineteen hundred hours, two days from above date. At that time, you will please inform Colonel Chatham that he is to be temporarily quartered at the Hotel International. You will also inform him that his presence is requested at a reception to be held in the Grand Ballroom, Imperial Palace, to begin at twenty-one hundred hours on the report date. Please find enclosed, etc., etc. Signed, Answar M. Faran, Aide-de-Camp to Field Marshal Yusuf ibn-Tashfin."

Khalifa glanced up. "Enclosed were a chit for a billet at the hotel, a formal invitation to the recepton and instructions on which tailor to see about your dress uniform. And that, Colonel Chatham, is the only illumination that I am able to cast on your mystery."

"I am to understand, then, Colonel Khalifa, that although I am assigned to your command, you have no idea why?"

"None whatsoever. I could not even hazard a guess. The only further assistance I am able to provide is to have one of my aides conduct you to the tailor mentioned and see to your other immediate needs."

"Thank you, Colonel." Chatham rose and accepted the envelope from Khalifa. "At this stage, it wouldn't surprise me if I were assigned as dance instructor at the military academy."

Chatham said his good-byes, collected the aide waiting in the anteroom, and left.

He glanced in the mirror one final time, still feeling like the student prince. With the high-necked, white dress tunic, gold-laced, red-piped shoulder boards, black riding breeches and polished boots, all that was missing was a Heidelberg dueling scar to make him the perfect Prussian junker.

From the commandant's office, Chatham was taken to the tailor who was standing by to get his measurements. Then he went on to the hotel where he was installed in an elegant, air-conditioned, three-room suite. By the time he had been served an early dinner, his completed dress uniform had been delivered to his door. He took his first adequate shower in months, finding a complete selection of expensive toiletries and shaving gear in the bathroom cabinet. He dressed in his new finery and rechecked the engraved invitation to make sure of the arrival time of his limo.

He still had a half hour to kill. He poured himself a scotch, neat, from the well-stocked bar and walked out onto the balcony. The lights in the square illuminated it poorly. Only his Imperial Highness, sitting on his bronze charger, was bathed in the harsh light of several spotlights. Chatham looked down, but the balcony overhang obstructed the view of the merc guards at the entrance. Being on the sixth floor, he could see over the roofs of the surrounding buildings to the palace lights in the distance.

He finished his drink and returned to the living room. He checked the room a second time but still found no bugs. It didn't mean much. If they used a wall spike or half a dozen other methods, nothing would be visible.

The phone rang and the desk clerk informed him that the limousine had arrived. He collected his gold-braided peaked cap and white gloves, then descended to the lobby.

The driver accompanied him past the guards to the gleaming black chariot with the royal crest on the plates. Recognizing him for what he was, the guards seemed stunned. The car pulled away and gained speed, the driver skillfully weaving through the sparse traffic.

They had to go through two checkpoints on the palace grounds, manned by mercs, before pulling up to one of the many entrances to the palace itself. From there on in, only Zakariyan soldiers were posted. Chatham entered the ballroom and could see why. Half the guests were foreigners. The Field Marshal was puting on his window display with a passion.

Chatham delivered his invitation to the wigged majordomo who allowed him in, obviously against his better judgment. The crystal chandeliers, marble floors, tapestries and rococo ornamentation oozed wealth and power. Chatham felt as uneasy about it as the majordomo.

He stepped to one side of the arched doorway to

reconnoiter this particular jungle before he plunged in. The foreigners—mostly journalists, business execs, diplomats and their spouses—were about what you would expect at any quasi-diplomatic function. Most of the Zakariyan men were in uniform, though they would never be mistaken for practicing soldiers. Overweight and/or doddering, their chests weren't big enough to contain the medals, decorations, and ribbons they sported. Chatham could picture them tripping over their swords and sounding like a hardware store in an earthquake when they hit the floor. Their women, except for several obvious mistresses, looked out of place in their too-tight formal gowns and gaudy jewelry. There were, of course, no Mpeche. A good part of the crowd was well on its way to falling-down-drunk.

Which, under the circumstances, didn't seem like a half bad idea. Chatham located the bar and aimed himself in its direction. He seemed to dampen the party spirit in every cluster of merrymakers that he neared.

He received a glass of scotch from a liveried barman and was just turning to face the circus when he heard a familiar voice.

"Chatham, old man! I didn't expect to see you again so soon!" He saw Freddy plowing awkwardly through the crowd with a drink in one hand and dragging a delectable little bit in his wake with the other.

And she was fine. Small, just the better side of five feet with a slim, boyish figure. Chatham never had been overly fond of high milk producers. Her hair was saved from being mousy brown by golden streaks that didn't come from a bottle. The shag cut was casual and, in this climate, pegged her as a practical woman. Her simple, white, floor-length sheath accentuated her deep tan. As she drew closer, Chatham spotted the minute wrinkles at the corners of her blue eyes, made more visible by her slight frown. Exposure to the elements and not age, was his guess. Without the slimming effect of the high cheekbones, her upturned nose and full lips would have given her face a babyish plumpness.

Freddy lurched to a halt, adding a few new liquor stains to the cuff of his white dinner jacket. "My, but you do get around, chum! Elana Christian, I want you to meet a good friend of mine, Colonel Erik Chatham. Elana's a freelance photographer, here to cover the unpleasantness. And, of course, no need to explain Erik's vocation.

The girl and Chatham exchanged noncommittal nods.

"Elana's an Aussie, but then, we can't all be British!" Freddy's grin dissolved in the silence. "That's a joke, don't you know."

"Colonists can't be expected to have a finely honed sense of humor." The vision's first words carried obvious sarcasm.

"Oh yes! Don't I know. Good heavens! The ambassador just arrived! I really must go and pay my dues! Be so good as to look after Elana, there's a good man. Have Erik tell you about the train ride, luv. It's simply a smashing story!" And just that quickly, Freddy disappeared.

"I wonder just how pleased the ambassador will be to see his young colleague," Chatham ventured.

"Oh, Freddy is quite harmless, so he's tolerated by just about everyone." Her defensive tone implied that the criticism was out of place.

"May I get you a drink?"

"No thank you. I don't drink at these affairs. It gives me the edge on budding Lotharios." So much for the liquor ploy. "What about the train?" They certainly were eyes you could happily drown in.

"Just a minor disagreement over right of way with some Mpeche."

"Lord save us, the strong silent type."

"Yup, bastard son of Gary Cooper."

"Gary who?"

He sighed for his wasted youth. "Just an inside joke."

"I dislike inside jokes." This cool young woman was starting to get on Chatham's nerves.

An angelic smile and twinkling eyes suddenly appeared. "I'm starting to bug you, right?"

"Did the trapped animal look give me away?"

The soft laugh was everything promised by the smile. "If I don't watch myself, I do that all too often. I don't always mean to. But it's my defense mechanism for the paper shufflers of the world."

"I can assure you, with all candor, that I am not now, nor have I ever been, a bureaucrat."

"And you are American, right?"

"Are my horns showing?"

"Do you realize that you have skillfully avoided

answering all my questions? It's scientific proof of a definite devious streak. No horns. I noticed on your blouse, along with the Ma'ribassan Cross of Gallantry with swords and Order of Merit, you're also wearing a Silver and Bronze Star with Oak Leaf clusters. American medals."

"In the Volunteers, you will also find a number of Croix de Guerres and even a few Iron Crosses thrown in. You didn't pick up medal identification as a fashion photographer."

"Correct, sir. What's a sweet young thing like you doing as a combat photog, please don't ask. I spent some time in the late, great Vietnam conflagration and spotted quite a few of those shiny trinkets they give away to madmen."

"I won't argue that. Where did you stay in the land of shining waters? Saigon, I suppose."

"Please. I said I don't get along with paper shufflers. When I got out of the boonies, I spent most of my time at Cam Ranh Bay up by the base of the peninsula. Even the mud and mosquitos there were preferable over the idiots in Saigon."

"Sort of out of your element here, aren't you?"

"You should talk. Unfortunately, I haven't got past the chairborne rangers yet. I'm kept busy trying to find the right doors to open to get a hook. As a matter of fact, you look more lost than I."

"All alone in the big city and no one to talk to. Maybe you could give me some hints on who and who not to avoid."

Elana turned and scanned the ballroom. He was aware of someone standing motionless behind him.

Against his instincts, he did nothing.

"Just about anyone you would need to know is here tonight," Elana began. "Let's see. First, over there by the pillar—the little, shriveled old man leering down that redhead's cleavage—His Imperial Highness, Emperor Khamlanadur. The only thing that keeps the old bird upright is the gold braid on his tunic. He likes young girls. It keeps his courtiers scouring the kindergarten set. Has a tendency to drool when aroused. He still thinks he holds power. The old duck plays with toy soldiers, too.

"Then, over there by the buffet, surrounded by all the earnest young men—not all attracted by political zeal, I might add—is the leader of the loyal opposition, Abd al-Mu'min al-Kumi. He's the short, stout man in the obsolete tux. He'd like nothing more than to take over. But, being a realist, he keeps a low profile and doesn't make waves for the regime. He knows he would end up slightly dead, or worse, in prison, if he bucked Tashfin. So he just bides his time."

"Speaking of Tashfin, where is my illustrious leader?"

"He will show up late, if at all. He throws these parties, then neglects to attend. He throws them partly to keep Papa Khamlanadur happy and partly because he digs the power scene.

"There are various other nationals, young Turks and officers, bought and paid for by one side or the other. But no one of importance. Now, as for the foreign diplomatic corps . . ."

"Hold up. That's enough for one lesson. My head in spinning already."

"Sure." She gave a crooked grin. "I've met your type before. Schmaltzmeisters, one and all. You probably took one look at the zoo parade tonight and pegged everyone, right down the line."

"Don't stop now. My ego is basking."

The beautiful laughter broke through again. "I think I will accept that drink now."

He clicked his heels and turned abruptly toward the bar, coming face to face with the silent shadow, as he had intended. Another Zakariyan colonel, slight of build, looked innocuous enough, except for the cold lizard eyes.

"Colonel Chatham." The choirboy voice was not framing a question. "I am Colonel Falan. Would you be so good as to follow me, please." And that certainly wasn't a request.

"Excuse me, Miss Christian," Chatham said to the puzzled beauty. "Duty calls. You must drink alone, for now."

"The meister strikes. And you asked me for lessons in who's who. But never mind. I'll be here when your duty ends." She looked at the ADC defiantly. "We can discuss the local fauna some more."

Chatham bowed and followed the already retreating Faran.

Walking up a wide marble staircase, they left the noisy hall behind. Then down a series of hallways, à la mad King Ludwig, past innumerable closed doors. Chatham marked his way with care. Know-

61

ing many lines of retreat is best, but even knowing
one is better than being lost.

Finally, Faran opened a door identical to all the
others on the floor.

"The Field Marshal will see you now," he said
and closed the door behind Chatham.

The room was a dramatic change, undoubtedly
to throw guests off stride. In contrast to the richness
beyond, the study was starkly modern and functional. The almost barren walls and sleek furniture
seemed transported from a Stateside corporation
executive suite. The deep red shag carpet, black
leather chairs, and massive desk lent solemnity.
The desk was bare: not a telephone, ashtray, or pa-
perclip to mar the polished expanse. And standing
to one side by a bookcase, leafing through a volume
with his back to Chatham, was Tashfin.

He put the book back on its shelf and turned. For
a tyrannical dictator, his appearance was almost
disappointing. There weren't any telltale movie vil-
lian clues like shaved head, gruesome scar, or mechanical hands that do heart transplants and open
beer cans.

The Field Marshal was disconcertingly average.
Average height with medium build. Gray hair, at-
tractively salt-and-pepper, cut conservatively. The
nose faintly prominent, but normal for an Arab.
Skin perhaps just slightly browner than the mean.
Face clean-shaven. Only his dress would set him
apart from his fellows. Other than the marshal's
crossed batons on his shoulder boards, the brown
army walking-out tunic and breeches were devoid

of military trappings. The austere hawk in the peacock run.

"Welcome, Colonel Chatham. I am pleased you could come." His voice was television anchorman smooth.

"Thank you, sir, but I wasn't aware there was any choice involved."

"Utter nonsense; I'm sorry if my subordinates left that impression, Erik. May I call you Erik?" Chatham nodded, but Tashfin didn't wait for the sign. He opened a desk drawer and pulled out a carved ebony cigar and cigarette box. He advanced, opening the lid. "Cigar or cigarette?"

He was gaining a feeling for friend Tashfin. With no ashtray or even wastebasket, he offered smokes. First the room, now this little move. The Generalissimo seemed fond of subtlety. It followed that he, in turn, admired that trait in others. It is always advantageous to induce your opponent to underestimate you. The role of a boorish, unmannered soldier for hire might do just that.

"A cigarette, thank you, sir." Tashfin lit his smoke and returned the box to the desk.

"Other than the unfortunate incident with the tribesmen, how was your journey?"

Chatham was willing to bet Major Mahadi's version of the "incident" was interesting, if not factual. "Sir, let's not waste my time or yours with unnecessary small talk. What exactly is the reason that you promoted me and had me reassigned?" Chatham punctuated the queston by tapping cigarette ash into the carpet. There was no visible reaction from Tashfin, but Chatham could swear he felt the temperature drop.

"An admirable American trait: directness. Since you desire it, then, I shall get to the point."

No chair had been offered so Chatham remained on his feet as Tashfin wandered over to the bookcase before facing him and resuming.

"You correctly surmised that both your promotion and reassignment were at my express orders. I have a special assignment to which I am giving top priority. I have been made aware of your exemplary service to my nation and felt that you were the one that could best carry out this mission. And the position called for an officer of command rank, hence your promotion.

"If I may speak bluntly, you are aware, as are many others in and out of this country, of the less than satisfactory reputation that certain units of the Imperial Forces have acquired."

Chatham waited until Tashfin glanced his way, then dropped more ash into the carpet.

"Much gossip is made of the 'hired guns' that are required to carry most of the weight in quelling the insurrection. Because of several unfortunate incidents in the past, the majority of the Imperial Army is considered less than professional. This is injurious to the morale of the Army and even that of the nation.

"For this reason, I am forming another regiment of paracommandos, the First. This regiment will be composed entirely of Ma'ribassan citizens and will be the élite unit of the Imperial Army. The First will take over the duties and responsibilities of the Second and will also conduct field operations along with the Third. Not only will the First be led and staffed by Zakariyans, it will be trained by them as well."

"That being the case, sir," Chatham interrupted, "I fail to see my place in the whole venture." This time he did detect faint signs of irritation.

"The staffing and specialized training of an entire regiment is a monumental task. I propose to accomplish it in three stages. First, prospective officers will be trained. They, in turn will train a larger body of noncommissioned officers. The officers and NCO's will then train the ranks. You, Colonel Chatham, will oversee the initial training of the officers. Any resources and support personnel that you require will be put at your disposal." Tashfin paused for effect. "Well, Colonel, what do you think of your assignment?"

"With all due respect, sir, bullshit," he said, dropping his cigarette butt to the floor and grinding it into the deep pile with his boot. Tashfin's face remained as immobile as Chatham's.

"Perhaps you would care to explain yourself, Colonel."

"Sir, I merely mean that is not the reason why I was brought here. It doesn't make sense. Accepting as fact that my meritorious actions were brought to your attention, nowhere in those actions is there evidence of outstanding training ability. I personally know of several mercenary officers who have an exemplary record as training officers.

"Secondly, if I may be equally as blunt as you, sir—" Tashfin curtly nodded his assent "—you know as well as I that our goal will never be realized. At best, your new elite regiment will be able to release the second for line duty. It will never carry out extensive field operations. The officers with any ability or connections will share the safe and flashy postings in the capital, while the ignorant and inept will be dumped in the bush. You will just be repeating the blunders made at the outset of your war. And you're much too smart to believe anything to the contrary."

There was a moment of silence and Chatham wondered if he had gone too far. Then Tashfin threw back his head and roared with laughter.

"Forgive me, Colonel, but you have no idea how refreshing the unvarnished truth can be."

"Thank you, sir. I thought I might save time and trouble. Which brings us back to the question at hand: why did you bring me here?"

"I was speaking the truth when I said that I have an important assignment that I feel you are uniquely qualified for. I want you to kill Mpanda Mhlangana. Or perhaps 'terminate with extreme prejudice' would be a better phrase."

This wasn't the time to talk, so Chatham rode it out in silence. Tashfin returned to the desk and this time came up with a file folder from another drawer.

"To save time, which you seem to value so highly, it would be well to dispense with your imminent and probably lengthy denials of your suitability. So please bear with me without interruption until I have presented my case." He paused for interruption but proceeded when none was forthcoming. "When you appeared in Brussels seeking employment, you caused quite a stir among my 'volunteer' recruiters. I have found that trained killers on the open market tend to be, for the most part, malcontents, deserters, misfits and psychotics. Under the circumstances, 'trained' is a loosely applied term. But then appears ex-Captain Chatham, trained in the United States Army Special Forces, forced to resign under a mysterious dark cloud.

"I must admit, I took a personal interest in you, Colonel. I sent my representatives, along with a substantial investigative fund, to the now defunct Republic of Vietnam, the site of your 'indiscretion.' Certain officials were quite talkative when approached in the right manner.

"I'm sure that the word 'Phoenix' has a special meaning for you. As with certain other Special Forces personnel, you were attached for duty to the Central Intelligence Agency's Studies and Observation Group, and further to the Phoenix Program as an 'advisor.' Quite simply, Phoenix was composed of assassination teams, provincial reconnaissance units, if you will. PRU's identified and eliminated the Viet Cong infrastructure. My source's estimate is that approximately twenty-thousand-five-hundred Viet Cong were neutralized from 1968 to 1971.

"You were functioning adequately, even with distinction. But then something went wrong for you. There my sources were hazy. It had something to do with the betrayal and destruction of your team. You hunted down the traitor, a high-level South Vietnamese official. The South Vietnamese wanted him dead. And he died.

"Barely saved from a legal lynching, you were expelled from Vietnam and forced to resign from the army. Why, I wondered, would a career officer knowingly throw away his future like that? But you have found a new home with us. And all I want is for you to assassinate one man." Tashfin stopped. It was Chatham's serve.

"Why bother? The Mpeche are no fatal threat. No matter who leads them, they can't overthrow your government with spears. They haven't even been able to break out of the lowlands in any substantial force. They haven't penetrated the plateau, much less the city. Another year and their back will be broken."

"You were intelligence officer with the Third. Have you noticed any recent trends in the bush?"

"Decreased enemy activity. Fewer contacts made. The main force must have retreated into the western highlands. I assumed that the high command was preparing operations to go in and get them, wipe them out once and for all."

"A logical conclusion. Except for this bit of intelligence. Three weeks ago, naval coastal forces spotted a small cargo boat aground near the mouth of the Western Kasambi. They investigated and were luckily able to capture one crewman, secure the boat, and retrieve a small portion of the cargo that had spilled into the bilge when the vessel ran aground. The recovered cargo consisted of about one thousand rounds of small arms ammunition, several anti-personnel grenades, and some C-4 plastic explosive.

"After a week of interrogation, the crewman—a city Mpeche—broke. The boat was one of three that was abandoned when it hung up on the bank. Its cargo was transferred to the other boats and we must assume that they reached their destination. The crewman was left behind to recover what he could, then destroy the boat.

"Other boats have previously made the run intact. We estimate that the Mpeche now have approximately two thousand automatic assault rifles, five hundred light and heavy machine guns, over a million rounds of ammunition, and unknown quantities of grenades and high explosives. And we can't estimate how much contraband has gotten through overland from the north.

"The main body of Mpeche warriors, male and female, has withdrawn to the highlands, leaving only a token rearguard to occupy the Third. This main body is now training with their new weapons.

"I needn't remind you, the Mpeche outnumber the Zakariya three to one. If they move in force, the government could topple. But they are still savages. Without the leadership of one man, they will disintegrate into squabbling clans. You must kill that man."

"No."

"What?"

"No, I won't do it."

"Of course, a bonus is involved. Besides your contracted wage, upon successful completion of the mission, fifty thousand dollars will be deposited in your Swiss account."

"It's not a matter of money."

A look of feigned disbelief played over Tashfin's face. "Can it be? The reformed whore enters the convent? The assassin tired of killing?" Sarcasm was replaced by bitterness. "Or is it something else entirely? When you kill for your homeland, it is justified; it is your duty. But when it is a banana republic whose fate hangs in the balance, a brown-skinned people who may be slaughtered by Communists, your sense of duty evaporates."

"Please, Field Marshal, please," Chatham sighed, "don't saddle me with qualities that I don't possess. I have a hard enough time trying to live up to the very few I have remaining. And don't bother raising the ante. It is simply too dangerous. A dead millionaire is still dead."

"But you are experienced. You have done it many times before. You can have anything you need, just name it."

"You can't give me the Phoenix organization. I have no backup, not enough intelligence. Why, you don't even know where Mhlangana is in the highlands, do you? What am I supposed to do, hike up and down the hills with a rifle on my back, hoping to stumble into the main camp? Then get a clear shot at the leader?"

"We could find the camp. I will have the air force scour the hills until we find it!"

"Your air force. What is it now? Ten F-86's and

twenty-five choppers? And when you scour the hills, the Mpeche will be alerted and will really bury themselves in the jungle. You can't see through trees."

"Then you refuse?"

"I'm as fond of money as the next man, but it is impossible. The odds are stacked against me living through it."

"I could give you a one hundred percent chance of dying," Tashfin said flatly. Chatham was wondering when it would come down to this. He hoped Tashfin wasn't overly emotional.

"If you mean you could have me wasted very easily, I agree. How does it go? 'And make it last a very long time, so that, in the end, you would beg for death.' To what purpose? Send me back to the bush. Let me smoke a few more enemies of the state before I buy the farm."

Tashfin laughed a second time, though not as heartily as before. "You are right, of course. Why uselessly waste your considerable talents? It is a pity. My solution would have been so simple. Now I must search for a more difficult one. But I will not send you back to the lowlands. You are now here, so you will initiate the training of the officers for the new regiment. We probably have several months before Mhlangana moves. Then I think the First will be badly needed."

Tashfin replaced the dossier in his desk.

"That will be all, Colonel. I have no further need of you."

"Yes sir, as you wish." Chatham walked to the door.

"You know, I think I now understand why you killed the traitor and threw away your career."

"And why is that, Field Marshal?"

"You killed many men, but strictly on orders, not indiscriminately. You were detached, aloof. It was only a job. But then your team was destroyed. Men you knew. You lost your detachment, you became personally involved. You struck back in revenge, knowing the consequences. Maybe loyalty is one of those few remaining qualities that weigh on you so heavily."

"You could be right, Field Marshal." Chatham smiled. It was a lie, of course. Tashfin was wrong.

CHAPTER FOUR

I won the battle the wrong way when our worthy Russian generals were losing it the right way. . . . Two of their colonels got their regiments driven back on the correct principles of scientific warfare. Two major-generals got killed strictly according to military etiquette. Those two colonels are now major-generals; I am still a simple major.

G.B. Shaw, *Arms and the Man*

Faran left him at the head of the stairs. The noise from the crowd had risen like a disturbed beehive. He could picture elaborate hairdos coming unpinned, gestures getting wilder, and the dancers clumsier.

Chatham had never been fond of drunken bashes, not being that much of a drinker himself. He got uneasy, felt threatened, not by the participants, but by the situation. Invariably, he rebuffed a high-class tart who thought she was sexy and wasn't, or laid out a tough guy who thought he could take him and couldn't. Minor hassles he didn't need and avoided if possible.

When he got on the floor, he could read further signs. The diplomats and businessmen had cleared the scene. Hassles were bad medicine in their line of work, too. The arena contained only potential combatants. He started to work his way around the edge of the herd, heading for the exit.

"Medals lie, Erik." He found Elana at his elbow. "I wait patiently by the bar, fighting off horny generals gunning for the little round-eye. When you finally do show, you beat a coward's retreat in the opposite direction."

"Would you believe I was circling for a flank attack? No? How about—I was looking for the men's room? No good? Then let's try . . ."

"You met the Field Marshal, he didn't like you, and you are going home to sulk."

"What makes you think that Tashfin wouldn't fall in love with me, Jack Armstrong that I am?"

Amusement sparkled out of her eyes. "Because you are too much alike."

"Is that a compliment?"

"It's too early to tell."

"I can give you time to think it over while I get you that drink."

"That's just what I don't need. My head needs clearing. How about an offer to walk me to my door at the Hotel International?"

"I'd be glad to escort you, but walking is out. Vermin appear after curfew. The streets aren't safe, young lady."

Even her small frown was attractive. "I detest these limousines kidnapped from some mortuary in Ohio."

"Your luck still holds. Colonel Faran has placed a shiny new jeep at my disposal. It should be waiting for us outside at this very moment."

"Wonder of wonders. Let us away, before the party moves into high gear."

They moved to the foyer and collected her evening coat and his hat and gloves. Elana also collected a battered camera that she said went with her everywhere. They set off in the jeep at a stiff speed, whipped by the cool night air. They left the lights of the palace and were swallowed up in the darkness created by malfunctioning street lights.

The wind made conversation difficult, so he navigated the deserted streets in silence and entered the square on the opposite side of the hotel. He glanced at Elana and saw her looking past the Emperor's statue at the hotel front. He followed her gaze momentarily, then looked back to the street. Then his eyes snapped back at the building.

Most of the hotel guests were still at the reception and had turned out their lights before leaving, as he had. The face of the building was dark, except for one patch of light on the sixth floor. Coming through the window of his room.

"Stop the jeep! Quickly!" Elana demanded.

He locked the wheels and as the jeep shuddered to a halt, Elana grabbed her camera and slipped onto the street. As she hiked up her long skirt, he asked her what the problem was.

"In the alley over there! I saw some blacks. Maybe I can get a picture of some rebels right here in Lamapur!"

Before he could step out of the jeep, she ran toward the alley, clutching her camera in one hand and holding up the hem of her cocktail dress in the other.

He shut off the engine and climbed out. He didn't like the looks of the black hole. And the guards at the hotel were still out of sight on the opposite side of the square. But, no guts, no glory. He was committed to the game even if he didn't like the rules. He trotted after Elana, who had already disappeared.

The blank-walled alley ran straight back for about twenty-five meters then made a ninety-degree turn along the rear of the building. The walls were seal-slick with moisture. He was alone.

He heard a muffled shriek from around the corner. He sighed in resignation. The cavalry was expected to charge to the rescue without reconnoitering the terrain, so he did.

He saw three figures as he turned the corner, at the end of a cul-de-sac. A sweaty, musclebound black was behind Elana, one arm around her throat and clutching a glinting *seme*, a two-edged Masai sword, in the other hand. A black centered in front of the struggling girl was busily turning her gown into rags.

Chatham paused to gather his thoughts and strategy but his mental energies were abruptly interrupted as two more Mpeche leaped from the shadows and pinned his arms. One on each side, they hustled him forward. He could smell the sweet odor of bhang, the sour smell of native booze, and the acrid bite of sweat. He struggled half-heartedly to test their grip, but gave it up. They were wary and left him no opening. Besides, he felt sharp steel pressed into the small of his back.

The amorous tribesman turned to face him and his grinning captors. When he spoke, flashing teeth filed to points, his English was so broken that he was barely understandable.

"White devil. Big man . . . kill Mpeche. Pah? I cut out your heart and piss on it!"

Chatham cowered convincingly, drawing laughs from the intoxicated warriors. From what he could see of Elana, her hopes of rescue were fading fast.

In dialect, the blacks discussed the problem at hand: whether to enjoy Elana before his eyes or to play it safe by cutting his throat before dessert. Without much hassle, the spokesman was convincing the others that Chatham could still be dangerous, even though he appeared to be a gutless wonder. Besides, if he were out of the way first, his two guards would be released to enjoy the white woman.

The talker turned his attention back to Chatham and hefted his *seme* ominously. He cowered back again and threw in some incoherent babbling for good measure. The grip on his arms was still tight but eased slightly as the blacks all roared with laughter.

When Chatham had ordered his custom boots earlier that day, the cobbler had been puzzled by his special instructions, but had carried them out none-the-less. He had attached metal cleats to the heels, which was normal enough. But first he ground down the outer edges to knife blade sharpness and tacked them on so that one-eighth of an inch of that edge was bared along the outer side of the heels.

Now, with the blacks distracted by the hilarity of the tough merc nearly doubled over in fear, he shifted his weight to his left leg. With practiced speed, he drew his right up until it almost touched his chest, then snapped it down. The cleat made contact with the first Mpeche in the flesh of the calf and laid it open to the ankle. He screamed, dropped his sword and clutched his leg, watching the blood well out of the evil-looking, but relatively harmless, gash. The cleats weren't meant to disable, only to distract.

Chatham was now held only by his left arm and had room to manuever. Before the wounded man's companions got over their shock, he delivered an outside standing kick with his left leg that caught the second captor on the outside of his knee joint. The power of the kick crushed the locked knee inward, popping cartilage and snapping bones. The Mpeche collapsed, whimpering, and crawled around in aimless circles like a dying chicken.

The first Mpeche had recovered his wits along with his sword. He stepped in close with a downward stroke aimed at Chatham's exposed neck. The merc's rising overhead block neutralized the blow, catching his attacker's wrist on his forearm. He left himself wide open for the upward elbow strike that followed. The point of Chatham's elbow struck him on the point of his chin, the transferred energy snapping his head back, breaking his neck. With the first two out of the match, Chatham turned his attention to the amorous talker.

He was cautious, having seen the elimination of the first two. He moved in the wide-footed knife fighter's stance with his *seme* well back out of reach. Chatham couldn't afford to wait him out, so moved in on attack.

An unarmed man moving to the blade rattled him and he lunged forward with the sword raised overhead. Chatham dodged inside the sword arm and deflected it with a knife hand block; then he threw the swordsman off balance and gave him a reverse punch to the face. Before he could recover, Chatham thrust forward with a powerful double-fist punch, both fists striking the rib cage in unison. As he fell, bright red blood gushed from his nose and mouth. His shattered ribs had punctured his lungs. Unconscious before he hit the pavement, he would shortly suffocate as he drowned in his own blood.

Chatham moved swiftly into the forward stance, facing the last opponent. The big black still had his grip around Elana's throat and, with a look of animal cunning, he tightened it. He brought his *seme* point up and rested it against the side of her throat.

"Let me pass or the white bitch dies, white dog!"

"Do your damnedest, you black pile of shit." Chatham smiled. "The slut means nothing to me. You die either way. Let her go, you die easy; harm her, you die slow." As he talked, he started easing closer.

The words confused the black man. White men didn't react that way and it threw him off balance. The only thing he was less prepared for was Elana's move. She shoved upward and sank her teeth into his forearm. He yelped and jerked his arm away in reflex. Elana let her body go limp. Her weight tore loose his grip and she fell to the ground, rolling quickly out of reach.

The Mpeche mistakenly kept his attention on his ex-hostage. If Chatham were sparring with an experienced karateka, he wouldn't have attempted his next move. It is easily blocked, leaving the attacker defenseless. But the blacks seemed only to know cut and thrust, and were not even adept at that.

He launched into a jumping front kick. His leap carried him over the three meters separating them at a height of five feet. He lashed out with his instep and caught the black in the throat. He landed on his feet as the native crashed into the brick wall behind him. Chatham stepped in close and, with a one-two motion, he threw a downward knife hand strike with his right and a driving knife hand strike with the left. Crushing contact with both collarbones snapped them like dry twigs. His arms dropped limply to his sides. Chatham stepped back to finish him off.

Elana yelled a warning and he spun around, letting the black slide down the wall to sprawl in an unconscious heap. Chatham dismissed him from his mind as he faced the new menace.

The Mpeche with the destroyed knee had recovered a heavy throwing spear. Obviously in great pain, he knelt stiff-legged about ten meters from Chatham, drawing back his throwing arm. He was out of reach and Chatham knew, even wounded, a Mpeche could be deadly with the weapon. Chatham prepared to dodge, the only option left.

As his arms started its forward motion, and Chatham's belly muscles tightened, the alley echoed with the muzzle blast of a high-velocity cartridge. The spear's tip harmlessly struck sparks on the cobblestones several feet in front of the black as he collapsed with half his forehead blown away.

From the shadows behind the corpse stepped a uniformed white, a smoking auto in his extended hand. He acknowledged Chatham with a nod, quickly checked out the other Mpeche, then turned back to the survivors.

"The spear chucker's dead, sir. Of the others, one's bought it, two just about. How about you and the lady?"

Elana, attempting to repair the major damage to her dress, said she was just shaken up. Being a gentleman, the young officer ignored her deshabille and kept his attention focused on Chatham.

"I'm all right, Lieutenant. But I wouldn't have been if you hadn't shown." It was an implied question and the man picked up on it.

"Lieutenant Blair, sir. I'm commanding the guard detail at the hotel. I thought I heard a vehicle brake sharply. I checked and saw it was army, so I came to have a look-see."

"Don't get me wrong, I'm glad of it, but wasn't it a little daring to come running in by yourself?"

"What you meant was, wasn't it a little foolhardy." Chatham took a liking to the young Irishman who spoke his mind. "Two rifleman are covering the entrance. They'll drop anyone coming out without the password. I thought it ill-advised to bring them in these close quarters." Chatham nodded, even more favorably impressed.

"I'll give you the code and you can see the lady to the hotel, sir. I'll clean up here."

Chatham ushered Elana to the street. As they passed the riflemen, positioned to catch the alley mouth in a cross fire, two pistol shots erupted from it.

Elana flinched, then asked incredulously, "He shot them?"

"They were too far gone to be of use for inter-rogation."

They drove up to the hotel entrance in silence.

He wandered around her suite, sipping a scotch. The battered camera she had carried into the alley lay on the desk with a shattered lens. There were several other cameras and paraphernalia packed in a shoulder bag also on the desk.

When they got to Elana's door, she had offered him a drink. Once inside, she gave him her order and disappeared into the bedroom to discard the ruined dress and repair other minor damage. He shrugged off his once immaculate tunic. It now looked as if it had been tie-dyed in a storm sewer.

Elana came back to the living room, and Chatham turned to hand over her drink. She was dressed in a floor-length blue hostess gown. Buttoned to her throat and falling straight to the floor, a sexual aura insinuated itself through the concealment. She accepted the drink, cool fingers brushing his.

"My dress is a complete loss. I can't afford much more of that." She hesitated and her gaze slipped away from his. "Sort of a stupid move, wasn't it?"

"For a sixteen-year-old, no; for an experienced combat photog, yes."

"I don't know what happened to my common sense. All the frustration of being held in Lamapur. . . . I just had to try to get a picture of the only rebels I might ever see. Don't be angry with me."

"I'm not angry. Bemused, perhaps, that your desire for a picture cost four men their lives. God knows, they meant less than nothing to me."

She moved in and clung to his chest. He would have given the performer top marks, except for the calculated move of carefully setting down the glass. The miracle fabric of the gown seemed to disappear as he felt her small form press against him, full length. When she spoke, the catch in her voice, muffled by his shirt, was masterful.

"I just realized; I owe you my life."

"You owe me nothing."

"But I do. If it hadn't been for you . . ."

He cut her off. "Accepting that, for the sake of argument, I hereby dissolve the debt. I rip up the note, obligation destroyed."

She stiffened, then dropped her arms and stepped back, looking up at him.

"You're some kind of bastard, aren't you? You don't make it easy. You just let me hang there and twist in the breeze."

He kept his tone impassive, didactic. "Life is precious, as I am all too well aware. Word games are just useless shadow-boxing. Time wasting. I find you very attractive, disturbingly so. Right at this moment, I can't think of anything I want more than to make love to you. If you feel the same, we can do without the pink satin bows and frilly pinafore."

"I wait all my life, and what happens? The white charger is mud-spattered and the armor needs a good going over with Brillo." She slowly undid the gown's top button. "Come then, my Lochinvar, to the main event."

The robe soon fell open, then whispered off her shoulders and drifted to the floor about her ankles. Dresden doll came to mind, but that was wrong. There was no hint of fragility, but that of compact, well-toned strength.

Slim neck, rounded shoulders, teeny-bopper breasts crowned by deep russet, aroused nipples, slender waist, swelling thighs and then again slim legs ending in tiny ankles and feet. Her figure was that of an athlete: slender without the starved mannequin gauntness.

By sleight of hand, her fingers undid the buttons then disposed of his shirt. She melted back into his arms. Their body heat mingled unobstructed and her breasts gently, insistently probed his chest.

No thought of attempting the bedroom. Feverishly, she helped him out of his clothes, then they sank down in the deep pile carpet. Her torso tingled on his chest and her thigh made contact with his groin, he could swear, causing sparks. The touching, exploring, tasting lasted an eternity. They coated each other in mingled sweat. He rolled, and she with him. At the end of the reversal, he thrust deep. Then time escaped, returning only when they collapsed and lay where they fell, exhausted.

The second time was legitimized by the double bed. And after, with the bedside table stocked with potables and smokes, he stroked her exquisite body, reluctant to release her even though sated.

Elana nestled in the hollow of his shoulder, rubbed his chest. She absently traced a nine-inch scar bisecting his pectoral.

"Was it painful?" Curiosity more than concern in her voice.

The moment that the Chinese infantryman had bayoneted him was blurred, half-forgotten. "Initially. Then the circuits overloaded and the numbness canceled the pain."

"You puzzle me. Frighten me, too."

"All soldiers do that?"

"I don't make love to all soldiers," she said with a scowl. She paused. "Don't you want to know why?"

"You're going to tell me anyway," he replied, stroking her shoulder.

"You're a violent man. Deadly. And yet, it is

cold, thinking violence. The pros I've seen, they're like vicious animals, genetic throwbacks. It's a wonder they're considered civilized. But you, you're different. If you were fighting for an ideal, I think I could understand. It's like man's humanity has been twisted in you."

"You're way off base on the true nature of man. There was once a dry, dusty little scholar; his name escapes me. He made a study of war. In the five thousand odd years of recorded history, he could find only about two hundred and fifty when there was not a major war going on somewhere.

"You speak of civilization, modern man. Lover, there is not one continent, right this minute, that doesn't have some dirty little war in progress. Man is a beast, worse than any other animal. He kills for the pleasure of it. Man's inhumanity to man is an integral part of us all."

Elana rolled onto her elbow, facing him. Her ripe, firm, distracting breast hovered near his face.

"I don't believe a word of that and I bet you don't either, really. Whether you admit it or not, you have to be fighting for something."

"I am. Money. And when I get enough, I'll retire from this veil of tears and buy me a monastery," he said as he tumbled her across his chest in a very nonmonastic manner.

She giggled, gave him a peck on the lips, then rolled away from him onto her back. "Is that what you discussed with your boss? Negotiating a cost of living raise?"

"Better. Tashfin wanted to adopt me as his bastard son and make me the Prince of Wales."

She laughed, but her voice was solemn when she asked, "Erik?"

"Yes."

"You didn't really mean what you said, did you?"

"Mean what?"

"In the alley. When you told that Mpeche that you didn't care if he killed me. You wouldn't have let that happen, would you?"

Chatham reflected that civilians have this idiotic habit of believing what they see on the telly and in the movies. Stock scene number 87: the bad dude is cornered by the cops; enter bumbling, beautiful hostage; bad dude places gun against beautiful hostage's head and orders cops to drop their guns. Which they do hurriedly, right? Wrong.

Elana looked like she had something else to say. He slid his hand down over her flat stomach. Her mouth opened but no words came, only a low moan.

"Of course I wouldn't let it happen, lover."

He didn't take the elevator from the second to the sixth. He wasn't being discreet for her sake. There were no gossips wandering the halls at 3:00 A.M.

Elevators are ideal traps. He once knew a fellow who took an elevator to the twenty-second floor. On the ninth, the doors opened and he was greeted by two blasts of double-o-buckshot from a cut-down alley gun. The surprise scared him to death.

He walked up the four flights, taking his time, feeling his way.

On the sixth floor landing he opened the door and glanced both ways. Except for the mandatory potted rubber plants, the hall was well lit and deserted. He walked softly toward his room.

He slowed up, moved to the wall opposite his door and froze. The door was slightly ajar and light from the room gleamed through the gap. Whoever had entered his room would be a damn careless fool to still be there. And yet . . .

He unbuttoned his tunic and retrieved his Walther PPK from the waistband in the small of his back. From the pocket, he took a metal cylinder about six inches long. He threaded the silencer on the slightly exposed muzzle. The 9-mm kurz is not, by itself, a man-stopper. Like hitting a man with the point of a pool cue rather than a bowling ball. He had added a little refinement to the high-velocity bullets. He had filled the hollow points with a little mercury. The Geneva Convention had outlawed explosive bullets. Too effective, he guessed. His little concoction would open up a fourteen-inch rat's hole, guaranteed to stop anyone. Or at least make him pause to reflect.

Even in the confines of a room, little more would be heard of the pistol than the metal click of the moving slide. If Tashfin had had a change of heart, and had sent over one of his bully boys, Chatham didn't want the mercs from the lobby interrupting.

He moved to the left side of the doorway, thumbing back the burred hammer. The long snout was poised. He placed his free hand gently on the door as he crouched. When the door came open, little more than the gun and his right eye would be visible at waist level. If company was waiting, a small target at an unexpected place would give him a fraction of a second's edge.

He took a deep breath, let some of it out, and pushed the door open. In a fluid reflex, his arm straightened, his eye lining the sights up on the chest of the occupant.

Freddy was facing him in a chair in the center of the room. He was still in evening dress, but had changed since Chatham last saw him. The foolish horseface was gone, the lower jaw seemed not to recede as much. The clown had been replaced. The metamorphosis itself was ominous.

He smiled. "Very good, very good. I didn't hear you coming and, believe me, I was listening."

"On the floor, spread-eagle. Move very slowly," Chatham said, gesturing with the silencer.

"Come, come, Erik. There's no need. I'm not armed."

"I won't say it again. Assume the position."

He shrugged his shoulders and followed instructions. When he was face down in the center of the floor, Chatham moved in and shut the door to the hall. Keeping Freddy in full view, he did a sweep of any possible hiding place. Satisfied that they were alone, he approached the Englishman from the rear.

Chatham frisked him while keeping the pistol out of reach.

"Well, well. Undersecretary of Economics, indeed. What's this, then, Freddy? A pocket calculator?"

He removed the Browning .32 from a jacket

pocket. With that pea-shooter, he'd be further ahead carrying a book of matches to give adversaries a hotfoot. There's no figuring individual taste, Chatham thought.

"Can I get up, now?"

"Sit in the chair you were in."

Freddy moved slowly without being told. Chatham removed the Browning's magazine and chambered round and pocketed them. He tossed the pistol across the room onto the sofa and pulled up a chair. All without taking the gun off Freddy.

"I'm disappointed in you, old bean. First breaking and entering. Then, not carrying heat, but lying to me about it as well. Not very diplomatic. Not very diplomatic at all. That seems like an apropos starting point. Commence explanation at will, Freddy."

Freddy was relaxed. They were both pros and knew it. No one would get hurt . . . accidentally. And Freddy wasn't about to make a move that would get him hurt intentionally.

"I intend to do just that, chum. After all, that's why I waited for you."

"You could have waited outside my door. Or even come during normal business hours."

"I didn't wait outside because I needed the time to check your suite electronically for bugs. And I didn't come at a more regular time because I don't want our meeting to be a matter of public record."

Freddy started to move his leg. Chatham's finger tightened. He froze, then continued slowly until he finished crossing his legs. He was testing just as

Chatham would have.

"My undersecretary role is my cover. Everyone in the capital knows it, of course. Except, perhaps, for the ambassador. He is continually harping on my cavalier attitude toward Her Majesty's business interests. I'm actually the S.I.S. resident, Chief of Station for Ma'ribassa." Freddy put on a mock frown. "Now you've punctured my ego. You don't even look surprised."

"I may not have known what you were," Chatham replied, "but I knew what you weren't. You weren't the befuddled dilettante your image projected. Following me into that Mpeche mob ruined your image." Freddy nodded in agreement.

"That explains your rather peculiar visitation rites," Chatham continued. "But it brings to mind a further question. Why do you want to talk to me off the record?"

"Do you mind if I smoke?"

"Not at all."

Freddy moved his hand toward his inside jacket pocket, but Chatham halted him with a twitch of the PPK. He took a cigarette and matches with his free hand and tossed them in Freddy's lap. He lit up.

"The matches, please."

He tossed them back. Chatham made no move to catch them, letting them fall on the carpet at his feet.

"Wary sort, aren't you?"

"Comes from watching movies."

"Believe me, I have no wish to cause you harm.

Quite the contrary, in fact."

"Oh, I believe you. Tell me again about not being armed."

"I hope you will forgive my little lies. Nasty habit of the profession, I'm afraid." He turned serious. "But what I am about to say is the truth. I need your help too desperately to risk lies. And I will get right to it," he said, glancing at his watch, "as the witching hour approaches.

"As you know, Tashfin's government is actively supported by H.M.'s, both economically and militarily. Realistically, this status quo is maintained in return for certain concessions: mining and drilling rights, mainly. Even your country has a finger in the pie. The latest little CIA bribe was a cache of wicked little antiguerrilla weapons complete with technician, still collecting dust in some warehouse.

"The British citizen has been force-fed shit like bulwork against Communism, shield of democracy, etc. It gets pretty thick around merry ole Parliament.

"Everything was cozy, but then Tashfin got greedier, as if his Swiss account isn't gigantic enough already. It's the same old saw: pay me more or I take my ball and play with the red brethren. Malta almost got away with the same extortion scheme not too long ago."

"But it didn't turn out exactly as Malta's PM wanted, as I recall."

"True. He did take a minor pratfall when we didn't play along. But that only involved a modicum of prestige and a naval base. Hell, we already have a base on the Island of Micramar—which is safely in international waters. The mineral rights in question are worth a bit more to 'Perfidious Albion.'"

"The solution, as I see it, is to get rid of Tashfin and replace him with a more sympathetic patriot," Chatham offered.

"Ah, you are way ahead of me, Erik. I'm pleased. Our first choice would have been Kumi. He carries with him a certain odor of legitimacy. But it would take a regiment of the Household Cavalry to put him in power and keep him there. Such an overt move is, sad to say, out of the question. Certain MP's have blithered on so much about Defender Tashfin to the unwashed masses that they can't reverse themselves now without sticking their heads in a bucket of their own shit. Even now, a shipload of munitions and armament is being collected in Birmingham and will arrive here within the month. As always, the Generalissimo will ride down in his yacht to meet the steamer. He will escort it publically back to Lamapur where we will all drink toasts of everlasting friendship."

"Mhlangana's men aren't a Guards Regiment, but it's the only game in town, right?"

"Bravo, Erik, bravo! Yes, if negotiations could be opened, our erstwhile young Turk might be just the ticket, even though he does seem a poor second to Kumi."

"So open negotiations."

"I've tried. Lord knows, I've tried. Two men's worth. The two messengers came back from the bush. At least their heads did. I think they were killed by the enlisted men before they delivered their salutations to the CO." Freddy stopped and looked Chatham in the eye. "I'm disappointed, Erik. You were doing so well up to this point."

"Don't go away mad, Freddy, just go away."

"But Erik, you're the best shot I've got. Although competent, my previous messengers were not exactly at home in the jungle. If anyone could get through . . ."

"Forget it."

"Before you make that final, let me at least mention the fee involved."

"Save your breath, Freddy."

"O my God! Diogenes, I have found an honest man. You've already taken Tashfin's shilling, is that it?"

"That's the second time this evening that I've been accused of being a better man than I am, Gunga Din."

"If not loyalty to Tashfin, then what?"

"*L'impossible nul n'est tenu.*"

"My public school French is a bit rusty, old man."

"A legal phrase. It means 'no one is bound to do the impossible'. Let me restate the obvious. A dead millionaire is still dead. For all you know, the message did get to García. Maybe the returned heads was his nibs' answer."

"What more can I say?"

"Nothing, other than have a good night's sleep."

He fetched Freddy's Browning, replaced the clip and handed it over.

"At least let's still be friends," he said at the door. "Don't call us. We'll call you."

It was late and Chatham was tired, but still he wanted to review the new information. He was doing just that, stretched out on the bed, smoking yet another foul-tasting cigarette.

First Tashfin. There was one bright spot. Like most men with absolute power, he imagined that power to be more effective than it was. His pride in the "complete Chatham dossier" was misplaced. A lot of effort and money was spent to discover only what was intended. Information that made Chatham out an unstable thug doing minor jobs for the Company. He evidently had not unearthed a whisper about Chatham's Omega infiltrations into North Vietnam, the KUBARK missions he organized, or his missions into Red China itself, leading Cambodian K's. It looked like his cover was still in place.

As for Miss Christian, she was a pretty good agent but she still had some rough edges. She slipped badly when she spoke of Cam Ranh Bay. The neck of the peninsula is one big sand dune, making it extremely difficult to be bothered by mud. And a fairly constant, stiff breeze off the South China Sea keeps mosquitoes away better than any netting. If she wasn't sure of her lie, she shouldn't have used it.

Chatham ruefully reflected that he was all too aware of his attraction to young ladies. He managed to meet his self-imposed quota. But it took a little bit more work on his part. When they throw themselves into his arms and/or bed at the first flash of his fruit salad, he turned skeptic.

Of course she worked with Freddy. In what capacity he didn't know. But she had gotten her orders fouled up somehow. When she saw the light in Chatham's room from the square, she hadn't known that Freddy was waiting to talk with him. She led Chatham off on the night run then kept him occupied in the sack to give Freddy time to escape undetected. As long as Chatham could keep his head while those around him were losing theirs, he'd let her hang around to pick his brains all she wanted.

Chatham had been at just such a point of no return many times. It always prompted the question of just what he was doing there. He had never been able to supply himself one simple, overpowering reason. There was duty, of course, for he did feel he owed an allegiance and service to his country. But he was inclined to dismiss that as a rationalization that was no longer fashionable. He was a good technician and successful at his chosen profession, but so were television repairmen. The thrills did not impress Chatham. He was by nature a cautious man, taking chances with the greatest reluctance, and then only when calculating the probabilities carefully. The glamour was dismissed out of hand by one who labored continuously to remain an unnoticed face in the crowd. Perhaps he was motivated by all or maybe by none. And he couldn't rule out that he was unconsciously lying to himself. That in turn made the entire one-man discussion an exercise in futility.

There was little left recognizable of the Midwestern innocent who entered the induction center so long ago. With no scars, inside or out, Chatham was just going to put in two years as an EM and part from the military, duty done. But, not satisfied with those superiors that would be responsible for keeping him alive, he accepted that in order to be the master of his own fate, he would also have to lead others. With no alternative, he signed up for OCS. Somewhere along the way to the lieutenant's gold bar, the world turned over and he knew he could never go back to the uncomplicated old life. He had been witness to too many deaths of good men in horribly absurd circumstances. To leave would be to turn his back and admit that the deaths had been all for nothing.

Like the natural pressure that turns a fragile lump of coal into a hard, cold diamond, Chatham's personal crucible exerted its own force. Not completely without his help. To survive in the arena, a man had to become as brutal and unfeeling as it was.

Chatham shook his head to clear it of the unproductive and slightly unsettling introspection, returning to the dangerous reality at hand. He could probably learn a bit more if he contacted the home office. But he was in deep cover and couldn't risk it. At least the players were starting to identify themselves. He wasn't flying blind anymore. On one wing and a prayer, maybe, but not blind.

CHAPTER FIVE

Remember: nine soldiers out of ten are born fools.

G. B. Shaw, *Arms and the Man*

He slept for six hours and got up rested. He showered and shaved. He ordered a light lunch from room service and made one other call to the 2nd Regiment HQ. He mentioned a few of the right names and got immediate attention to his requests. He was dressed in a new set of starched tiger fatigues by the time lunch arrived.

The lunch was barely finished when there was a knock at the door. He put down the list of necessities he had been composing and opened it.

"Come in, Lieutenant Blair, and make yourself comfortable."

The Irishman entered, bewildered, sweeping off his beret and tossing it on a lamp table. He was older than Chatham remembered. From his graceful way of moving, Chatham had taken him to be in his mid-twenties. His compact body would be

the envy of any high school linebacker. But his red
hair had a few strands of gray at the temples and
the face carried its complement of hairline
wrinkles. Chatham now guessed his age at between thirty-five and forty. Chatham gestured to a
chair and he sat.

"Can I offer you anything, Lieutenant?"

"Something cold to drink would be fine, sir."

"Iced tea all right?"

"Yes sir." He lit up a noxious local imitation of a
cigarette. He wasn't cowed by his surroundings.
That might be important later. Taking the tea, he
sat patiently waiting for Chatham to begin.

"Sorry to take up your free time after pulling
duty most of the night."

"That's all right, sir. Garrison duty is boring as
hell. This is the high point of my week."

"I might be able to change that for you."
Chatham saw a spark of interest light his eyes. "But
first I want to know about your background."

Blair stiffened. "I am not required to discuss my
past with anyone." He pointed to the tattoo on his
right forearm.

"Legio Nostra Patria," Chatham read. "Admirable tradition of the Legion, no questions asked.
And pardon the hell out of me for trampling on the
gentle feelings of a sweet young schoolgirl." This
brought a crooked grin to his weathered face. "But
I have to choose the right man. Since I can't afford
to judge you in action, I must find another way.
Knowing your experience will help. If you don't
want to play patty-cake, I'll look elsewhere."

"Well, now that you explained the question, that puts a whole new light on it. I was born Sean Blair to members of the Northern Irish peerage. Though of the nobility, my parents were of modest means—"

"Skip the bullshit, Lieutenant. You know what I want."

"Yes, sir." He wiped the smile from his face but his voice retained a trace of humor. "I attended Sandhurst, took parachute training, then was gazetted to the Eighth Queen's Royal Irish Hussars Armored Regiment.

"Later, I resigned my commission and joined the Legion, eventually being assigned to the First Paratroop Regiment. I spent several years fighting the fellagha in Algeria, rising to the rank of color sergeant. After the unsuccessful push against De Gaulle, the First REP was disbanded for its part in the revolt. I joined Degueldre's OAS Delta Commando. But when I found out what bloody butchers they were, I left them. I've been more or less in combat ever since then. Mostly squalid little affairs, but it's kept me in shape."

He halted his monologue, but, finding no satisfactory conclusion, he added, "My professional career in one breath."

"You seem well qualified. From the brief conversation I had with your superiors, they confirm. I think you are the man I want. Just one point. What was your reason for leaving the British Army?"

Chatham saw him blanch, seeming to be almost on the verge of being physically ill.

"No need to answer that," he continued. "It was just to satisfy my own curiosity."

Blair hesitated, obviously fighting a private battle. He seemed to resolve the conflict. "I understand. Still, I'm going to tell you. For the life of me, I can't explain why. You can call in the next candidate when I finish." He lit another cigarette with a rock-steady hand.

"I was accused of being a card carrying homosexual," he said straight off. He looked at Chatham with more than a trace of defiance. "It was true, of course. I always kept my 'activities' separated entirely from the service. But after I was found out, the pressure was there. If I had been in the ranks, I probably would have been discharged or beaten shitless by my mates. As it was, I was given the silent treatment by my fellow officers. There was no future in it, so I left."

He took a deep drag on his smoke. "And before you ask, yes, I still am a fag. I play my game with consenting adult partners whenever I can, outside the army. It's a poor choice to mix business with pleasure, so to speak."

He crushed out the half-smoked cigarette and began to rise. "Without further ado, I will take myself off. I would appreciate it if you would keep confidential what—"

"Sit down, Lieutenant," Chatham cut him off. "Personally and professionally, I could care less if you screw chickens. As long as you complete the mission assigned. If you can play grab-ass with half the troopers in your company and still get the job done, that's all I care about. Unless you've got something else on your mind, we'll get on with it."

Blair sat down with evident amazed relief.

"I'll give you an overview of what has to be done, then we can hash out the details. Field Marshal Tashfin is forming a Zakariyan para-commando regiment. I'm supposed to train the field grade officers, and they will take over from there. You will be my exec and TO. We could use a couple more TO's, but I want to keep it small and simple. We'll need a training camp and facilities for a company of about a hundred. You look like you have doubts. Spit it out."

"You were planning on full commando and para-chute training, sir?"

"That's it. No milk run."

"I think we won't keep them long. When it gets rough I think they will quit."

"We'll lose a few, yes. The normal amount of washouts. But the rest will stick with it. With a new regiment, the opportunities for graft and kick-backs are almost too good to be true. With all the new equipment flooding in, a killing can be made on the black market. And that's not counting the forced kickback of the troopers' wages and selling part of their rations. There's a fortune to be made. No, we'll have them kicking and screaming to get in and, once there, it will take a major offensive to dislodge them.

"I want a training camp far enough out in the boonies to rough up the recruits. Any ideas?"

"There's an armored unit about twenty-five

miles west of Lamapur, and some pretty rough terrain in the surrounding area. The barracks are in fairly good shape. Your main problem will be moving the tankers out."

"That's no problem. We've got priority rating. I'll put the word out and get them moving."

"Sir, don't misunderstand. At least I'll be doing more than I am now. But playing nursemaid to a herd of Zakariyan bluebloods isn't a hell of a sight better."

"Everyone has to start somewhere, Lieutenant. And there is the distinct possibility of moving up to bigger and better things.

"First things first, though. I've been making some notes on necessities. Let's go over it and see what you can add. Then we'll start kicking ass and get this farce on the road."

The next month was busy, but time still dragged slowly, waiting for an opening in Tashfin's armor. Days were spent with Blair and the native officers. And those few nights when no training was scheduled, Chatham spent with Elana. Most of the free time was savored in the privacy of her suite. Occasional free days were used lazing around the hotel pool in the sun. He heard they were the talk of the town. She spoke of her futile attempts to get out of Lamapur. He spoke of how the training was progressing. They each doled out their lies in turn and on cue.

The training had turned into a mess, as he had anticipated. It began on the first day.

Two days after the organization meeting, Blair and Chatham inspected the newly-deserted camp. The vacation orders for the armored unit had been hastily drawn up and executed. The barracks were full of refuse but would house over two hundred men when cleaned up. In comparison, the parade ground and empty vehicle park were fairly clean, only because the wind swept them morning and evening.

Except for the addition of a hurriedly built obstacle course and small jump tower outside the barbed wire perimeter, the camp sat unchanged in the middle of nowhere with only a rocky tor about three miles away for company.

Blair followed Chatham in the midday heat with a pad, making notes of changes and improvements that Chatham wanted. His experience as an officer and NCO made him invaluable. After the planning session, armed only with Chatham's authorization papers countersigned by the commandant, he had obtained all of the necessary equipment and labor, through legitimate channels and otherwise.

They had just finished the inspection and were having a smoke on the orderly room veranda when they sighted dust on the horizon. Fifteen minutes later the five-truck convoy rolled to a grinding halt on the parade ground enveloped by its own dust storm. Native officers tumbled out of the tarped deuce-and-a-halfs with their baggage, looking around in mixed anticipation and bewilderment.

"Get them into four ranks," Chatham said to Blair. "I'll make my debut when you have them squared away."

"Yes sir," he answered and moved off toward the milling mob as Chatham entered the orderly room.

He was attaching a roster to a clipboard when he picked up angry shouts. He moved back to the veranda. The Zakariyans were still in an undisciplined crowd, now surrounding Blair and in an obvious foul mood. A familiar figure was facing Blair doing most of the talking, supported loudly by the others. The yelling gradually died as Chatham approached.

"What seems to be the trouble, Training Officer Blair?"

Blair had not lost his composure. He had dealt with native officers before.

Before Blair could answer, the ringleader muscled him aside and shouted, "I demand to know who made the transportation arrangements!"

"Ah, Major Mahadi. What a pleasant surprise. I made the arrangements. Was everything to your satisfaction?"

"It most assuredly was not!" His tone had lowered, but not much. "Do you realize that over a hundred officers, some of them field grade, were crammed into those trucks and subjected to heat, dust, and every damned pothole between here and Lamapur?"

"Is that all?"

"No it is not, sir! There were no vehicles assigned to transport our baggage! We were forced to travel with our few personal items in these duffel bags rammed between our legs the whole way! I demand that these vehicles be sent back for our baggage and the senior officers' batmen immediately!" He stood defiantly, chin outthrust, his fists rest-

ing akimbo on his hips next to those god-awful
ivory-handled wheel guns. Chatham waited and
the murmurs died out.

"If you will please get into four ranks, I will ad-
dress myself to these and any other grievances."

Behind Mahadi, Blair's eyebrows raised briefly at
Chatham's soft reply. Mahadi stalked disgustedly to
the front of the orderly room followed slowly by the
rest. With maximum jostling, four uneven ranks
evolved.

"Here we go," Blair said under his breath as they
paced to the veranda. Protesting murmurs rippled
through the gathering as Blair and Chatham took
up positions.

"Gentlemen. Please bear with me while I discuss
a few elementary rules of this camp before I attend
to personal problems." They gave their attention
grudgingly.

"The purpose of this camp, as I am sure you realize, is to produce qualified officers for the new
paracommando regiment. Field Marshal Tashfin
has given me sole authority to conduct this advanced training as I see fit. For those of you who
may doubt this, a copy of those orders are posted on
the door of the orderly room. I mention this merely
to emphasize that any decisions made here by me
are unappealable." Chatham began to strip the
softness from his voice.

"This is not to say that you are bound to accept
these decisions. You are free to voluntarily terminate your training at any time, now or in the days
to come. I will feel equally free to terminate train-

ing when I feel it is necessary.

"Immediately after this formation, those wishing to terminate may obtain transportation back to the city on the vehicles that brought you. With any subsequent termination, you will provide your own transportation. If a steady pace of three miles per hour is maintained, the hike to the capital should take approximately eight hours." Incredulous expressions blossomed in the audience.

"At the commencement of training, there will be only two ranks: that of training officer and candidate. Training Officer Blair and myself will be addressed as such at all times. Our orders will be obeyed at all times. For those of you choosing to remain, you will find fatigues, minus any rank badges, in the barracks. You will change into these at the end of this formation, and your personal uniforms and baggage will be returned on the vehicles. You may retain your toilet articles.

"Which brings me to the facilities provided at this camp. The shower hall will be off limits at all times except for one hour every three days. Each trainee will be allotted one gallon of water per day. This gallon will supply you with your drinking water and any bath or laundry water that you require.

"As for meals, unfortunately, we were unable to obtain the services of a cook. In consequence, all meals will be field rations. You may heat your supper meal while present in the compound if you so wish. Anyone missing the designated meal periods, thirty minutes in length, will go without.

"The training load, of necessity, will be heavy.

You will receive instruction in the finer points of counter insurgency warfare. This will include training in special weapons and tactics, hand-to-hand combat, unarmed combat, map reading, radio procedure, and parachute training. Each dawn, after formation, we will take a run to the outcropping three miles away. Training Officer Blair and myself will eat our breakfast upon return. Anyone not returning with us will not eat. Training Officer Blair and myself will perform every exercise that you do. The only difference will be, of course, that we will do it infinitely better.

"From beginning until completion of training in about four weeks' time, trainees will be confined to the compound except when otherwise instructed.

"A further list of Company Orders is posted on the orderly room door. Infraction of any order will be grounds for immediate termination.

"In every possible phase of training, we will strive to maintain the realism of actual combat conditions. With that aim in mind, I was of the opinion that your temporary quarters should be a slit trench lined with a ground sheet. Training Officer Blair, a kindhearted soul, prevailed upon me to house you in the barracks. As with most comforts granted to you in the coming weeks, you must earn this privilege. For those choosing to remain, you have one half hour at the conclusion of this formation to change into fatigues and load the excess baggage. You will then be allotted an additional hour in which to thoroughly clean your living quarters. We will then have a recreational period at the obstacle course. While this is in progress, Training Officer Blair will inspect your handiwork. If he is satisfied, we will serve dinner."

Chatham turned to Blair and saluted. "Training Officer Blair, dismiss the formation." He returned to the orderly room while the Irishman took over.

Several minutes later, Blair rejoined him. "You should have seen the look on Mahadi's face," he laughed.

"I've seen the look before, thank you."

"I think we'd best watch our backsides while in the vicinity of that snake."

"That's why there are two of us, Training Officer Blair."

That day, three of the one hundred twenty-seven left on the trucks. In the following week, two more went, one with a compound fracture of the leg. Most of the trainees were company grade, young and fit, and managed to survive the backbreaking exercise. The two whites forced the men past their own endurance limits. They had the most trouble getting them to face and overcome their fears. And the cliff ladder was responsible for a good portion of it.

One morning, about midway through the first week, Chatham ran the men out to the cliffs while Blair drove a truck loaded with the day's rations and training equipment. After the Spartan breakfast, he took a company while Blair instructed the rest on booby traps. Chatham worked it so that Mahadi (who was in his group) would be one of the first to try everything. Chatham double-timed the company to The Cliff.

It was about three hundred feet high with wicked boulders crouching at its foot. An iron ladder, two feet wide, lay against it almost perpendicular to the ground. It was secured only at the top, which caused it to vibrate furiously when the slightest weight was applied. Chatham drew the men up and gave them a change to crane their necks.

"A simple exercise, gentlemen. You will notice the ladder and, of course, the cliff. I draw your attention to the rope running back to the ground at a thirty-degree incline from the top. That is for your benefit. After the exhausting trip up, you can rest coming down."

There was a general clearing of throats, licking of lips, and shuffling of feet.

"I will run through it for you once. If I can do it with this," Chatham said as he slung the Sterling machine pistol on his back, "you know it's got to be a piece of cake."

"Then maybe I should carry one, too," Mahadi snapped.

"No, Hop-A-Long, you'd just catch your thumb in the breech and I didn't bring my first aid kit."

The resulting snickers didn't improve the major's mood.

Chatham trotted to the ladder and started up, moving fast. The hot metal started to pitch like something alive. By locking an arm and a leg around the back of the ladder, he could move up while maintaining a secure grip. The smart ones below would watch and learn.

At the top, he snapped a wooden T-handle over the rope. He stepped into the void, bringing his legs together, flexed at the knees paratroop style. He rode the rope for its full length, hit and rolled as his legs took the initial shock of impact. He dusted himself off and strolled back to the waiting trainees.

"As I said, simple. The ladder's easy, just one foot over the other. One thing to remember about the rope: ride it to the end, gentlemen. Training Officer Blair has gone to great expense to provide nice, soft sand for you there. But in between, are very sharp, very hard rocks. Take the shortcut and you will positively hate yourself in the morning."

He slapped the wooden handle into Mahadi's stomach. "You first, sport." Mahadi tucked it into his belt and started up.

He went up slowly but steadily. He had watched Chatham and kept his body pressed close to the metal. He got halfway up and stopped, swaying like a pendulum.

His voice floated down weakly. "I don't think I can make it."

"Sure you can," Chatham shouted back. "You've done well so far. Don't look down, just keep moving."

"I don't . . . Please! . . . If you could come up and help—"

It was the pleading that made up Chatham's mind. Mahadi would hang by his thumbs before he begged Chatham for help. He hadn't had any trouble to that point. Anyone else up there, Chatham would have gone up and herded him to the top. Chatham unslung the machine pistol and worked the charging lever.

"I'll send my assistants instead," he shouted.

Mahadi looked down over his shoulder as Chatham snapped the folding stock out. Chatham raised it to his shoulder and carefully squeezed the trigger. The gun bucked in his grip as it spat out the 9-mm slugs. The burst hit the stone face about five feet below and to the right of Mahadi in a satisfying eruption of gravel and lead. For training, Chatham had loaded the magazines with soft, unjacketed lead bullets. They disintegrated or deformed on contact, lessening the chance of injury by ricochet.

His finger tightened again but another shot wasn't necessary. Mahadi scampered up the ladder faster than he had covered the first half. Chatham folded the stock and reslung the weapon as Mahadi came down the rope. The major rejoined the group white-faced, but said nothing. Chatham accepted the handle and tossed it to the next man in line.

"Time's a-wastin'. We can't monopolize all the fun things. Besides, when we finish, we have to do it all over again."

They only lost two on that day. One simply refused to go up the ladder, and one dislocated his shoulder and tore the ligaments in his knee.

As training progressed, interest started to pick up. The young officers hardened their bodies surprisingly fast. The obstacle course and exercises like the ladder gave them confidence, and with it, a certain amount of pride. It was then that Chatham had then turn in their fatigues for tiger suits and jungle boots.

The firing range was a trail that wandered through scrub brush and boulders. Targets popped up at random, teaching instinctive quick-kill firing. Chatham lost another man when, on the run, he tripped and put a rifle slug through his leg.

The hand-to-hand course consisted of relaying to the trainees all Blair and Chatham knew of dirty fighting. Which was considerable. They taught them how to make their own weapons, like a garrote from a length of piano wire strung between two sticks for handholds. Then they showed them how to use the garrote so that they could decapitate a sentry as easily as slicing cheese.

Chatham had scheduled parachute training for the fourth week. He contacted Colonel Khalifa to request aircraft, pilots, and 'chutes. He was informed that the requests were denied. First, because the aircraft were being used elsewhere. But mainly because the trainees were too valuable a commodity to risk by falling out of the sky. He argued, but Khalifa remained resolute, saying that the orders had emanated from Tashfin. Word of Chatham's casualty list had gotten out and influential relatives had put pressure on the Generalissimo.

Actually, Chatham was surprised that his training methods hadn't caught more flack. Still, Blair thought it amusing that they were to train qualified parachutists who never set foot on the deck of an airplane. They improvised by driving a truck around the parade ground letting the trainees bail out of the tailgate. "Advanced" training was held in the jump tower and cliff rope.

Chatham had planned an actual mission for graduation. So in the middle of the fourth week, he issued the troops their red berets, against his finer instincts. He gave them a two-day pass to Lamapur to let them strut around town in their new, and largely unearned, finery, hoping it would get them in the proper mood. He had to go to the city to coordinate final arrangements. Trucks took the officers while Blair drove Chatham in a jeep. He released Blair at HQ and the rest of that day was used up tying various loose ends. Business out of the way, he headed for the International.

The dirt road wasn't in the best of shape, but still they were making good time. Since they were nearing the sea, a cool breeze blew in their faces. It rippled through Elana's hair and carried the jeep's dust trail harmlessly from them.

Elana was in a good mood. After last night's preliminaries, he told her he had the day free and asked if she wanted to take a trip to the coast. She said that she was thrilled that she could escape from the city, if only for a day. When he picked her up in the morning, she brought a picnic lunch with her.

The road paralleled the river on the bluffs above it. The day was bright and sunny. Elana said that today, she even loved the sight of the sluggish, muddy-brown water below. Compared to the garbage-swollen stretch that ran through Lamapur,

Chatham supposed she had a point. She chattered gaily, losing half of her words to the wind.

The scenery was that of the rest of the plateau country: rolling grassland dotted occasionally by small copses of trees. On the riverbanks and bluffs, it was greener with thicker stands of trees. Dingy channel buoys bobbed on the water's surface to mark the safety of the dredged passage for incoming ocean vessels.

The bluffs gradually rose and with them, the road. Near the crest of a hill, a warning sign declared a restricted area ahead.

"What's that all about?" Elana asked as he slowed the jeep.

"Old coastal gun emplacement built by the imperialistic British to guard the river mouth. The naval artillery was removed quite awhile ago. Now it's manned by paras to discourage rebel infiltration."

They passed over the crest. A quarter of a mile down the road and fifty meters off of it, the concrete bunker perched on the edge of a bluff. The large firing slots, out of their sight, brooded over its flowing charge. Several off-duty mercs lounged around open steel doors within the wired perimeter. The rest of the contingent were out of sight somewhere in the squat two-story shelter. With the doors buttoned up, it became a giant, immobile tank. Built to withstand bombardment from the sea, it could shrug off anything the rebels could put up.

A flimsy wire barrier stretched across the road

anchored to a sandbagged guardpost manned by
two paras. The NCO casually motioned Chatham
to halt and walked to his side of the jeep.

"Sorry to trouble you, sir. I can see who you are
as well as the next. But it is SOP. I gotta see your
papers."

"That's all right, Corporal, I understand." He
fished out his ID and handed it to the man. "I'm
Colonel Chatham and this is Miss Christian. Do you
require her identification, also?"

"Not if she's with you, sir." Chatham caught
Elana's smirk from the corner of his eye.

"We thought we would take a holiday to the
coast. That's allowed, isn't it?"

"Right you are, sir. This point is for traffic goin'
the other way. We bottle up the peninsula. When
the tide is in, it's possible to land shallow draft
boats on the south side, and we stand guard there,
too. But when the tide's out, like now, the mud will
stop them so we just sit it out at the point here. It's
a long way to Lamapur, but the niggers could try
it." After a cursory glance, he returned Chatham's
papers.

"Must be pretty boring duty, way out here?"

"Oh, not so bad. It's all on rotation. The Second
Battalion has it now. C Company is on for the rest
of the month."

"The emplacement covers the whole river?"

"Right. We have four 106-mm recoilless rifles
mounted in the bunker. With their range, we can
cover anything on the water up to the opposite
bank. Using HE instead of armor-piercing, we can

do a number on a pretty good-sized boat. Anything too big for us and we just radio for air support. They can scramble in the city and be here in thirty minutes."

"Well, we'll probably see you when we go back."

"Yes, sir." The para moved the wire for them to drive through.

"Why all the questions?" Elana asked.

"A crown prince must know such things if he is to rule his people fairly and well," he said haughtily.

"All right for you, Casimir," she laughed. "When do we get to the beach?"

"Isn't one in the whole of Ma'ribassa. The coast is just swampy marshes or mud flats. Here, the cliffs fall right into the sea."

"Well, that tears my chance to take a dip and reinforce my tan."

"I didn't notice that you packed a bathing suit."

She wrinkled her nose at him. "A merc afraid of a little skinny-dipping?"

He grinned back. "Well, nobody 'splained it to me. Who needs water?"

The land started to slope down and was covered with a thin forest. Over the treetops, they got their first glimpse of the blue ocean stretching to the low horizon. He parked the jeep in the shade.

"The cliffs should be close by. Let's take a hike and see what we can see," he suggested.

Elana clapped on a floppy straw hat and sunglasses and joined him as he started off downhill.

The tree line ended without warning and they stood at the edge of a cliff that fell a hundred feet to the sea. Actually, a hundred feet to the mud. Without tide water, one mile of noxious, black mud was exposed and baking in the sun.

"Let's see if we can find a way down."

"The first question that pops into my mind is," Elana declared, "why on earth would anybody want to go down?"

"Who knows? This might be the perfect spot for my new mud bath health spa."

Elana sighed resignedly. "All right, Prince, I'm right behind you."

She followed cautiously as he picked his way down. The incline wasn't as steep as it looked from above. The deteriorating face was so clogged with broken boulders that it provided relatively easy climbing. The only casualties were Elana's safari jacket and slacks. Evil-smelling slime transferred itself from the rocks, liberally spattering her clothing. The stench from the flats was overpowering and seemed to soak right into the skin.

"We'd better get out of here before the scent gets to be permanent."

"That's a relief," Elana responded. "I was worried that you might want to wallow in the nasty goop."

"It's your glass house that looks the worse for wear, my dear," he said, pointing to her once-smart outfit, "not mine."

"The next time you ask me for a date, remind me to get my wet suit back from the cleaners."

It was easier climbing back up, and they were soon strolling back through the shade grove.

"What's that?" Elana asked, stopping him with a hand on his arm.

"What's what?" He hadn't heard anything out of the ordinary.

"It sounds like running water."

"Oh, that. There's a spring over to the left. I heard it on the way to the cliffs."

"Water! Maybe I can salvage something of the mess you got me into. Lead on, MacDuff, and devil take the hindmost!"

He pushed through the screening brush and, as they broke through, Elana gave a yelp of pleasure. The spring, bubbling out of some rocks about six feet high, cascaded down into a clear, waist-deep pool. The surrounding trees and bushes formed a quiet secluded refuge while permitting sunbeams to dapple the rippling water. Elana slipped past him onto the gravel verge and shrugged out of her jacket.

Her lithe, naked back started to affect him in uncontrollable ways. She put her blouse on a flat rock at the water's edge and, just as quickly, it was joined by her boots and slacks.

"That particular state could be dangerous in the light of the glances you were getting from the mercs up the road. They've probably got patrols out searching for you right now."

"You mean they would bother a lady just innocently doing her laundry? I would, naturally, expect you to provide a little protection," she said over her tanned shoulder.

"I doubt very much if an armored column would be of much help in that respect."

She turned and her panties slid down her thighs to dangle provocatively from one tiny foot, before they too dropped on the pile of clothing. She walked to him and pulled off his beret, tossing it over her shoulder.

Her fingers played with the top button of his tiger suit as she breathed, "Get out of those clothes. We'll go for a swim later."

"If I get out of these clothes, it won't be to get wet."

"Whatever," she said softly.

With all those rocks, you would have thought they couldn't find a comfortable spot.

They did take that swim after all. The water was cold, but with a little effort, they did get each other squeaky clean sans lather.

They lay in each others' arms in a large patch of sunlight, the sun and breeze drying both them and her clothes. He was drowsy, but prepared for her inevitable inquisitory pillow talk.

"Mmm, my great tawny beast of war," she said from the hollow of his shoulder. "A panther. Is that what you would choose for your totem? A fearsome cat to petrify your enemies?"

"No. A shark, I think."

"A shark!" she shivered. "How could you expect me to cuddle up to a slimy fish?"

"But for a fearsome totem, there's nothing better. He glides out of the murky, esoteric, primeval sea—an experienced killer since prehistory. In and of itself, the totally efficient death machine is bad enough. Then add its utter unpredictability. It attacks in the rain and sunshine—off crowded beaches or seventy miles upriver from the ocean. It attacks in depth of a hundred feet or will slide into three feet to snap at waders. It attacks a crowd in a blood frenzy like a meat grinder gone mad; or selects one swimmer, attacking again and again while ignoring a dozen companions. It has been known to leap into a boat to get to its prey. And it is horribly cold and emotionless. It moves in silence, offering no warning or explanation for its ferocity. Yes, definitely the shark."

She shivered in his arms again, then abruptly switched topics. That was not unusual in her covert search.

"It is times like this that I think I could just take up squatters' rights in this place and happily become a hermit."

"A hermit, by necessity, is alone, lover."

"Of course, certain rule changes would have to be made," she explained languidly.

"Well, good, that is one thing I am proficient at."

"Aren't you ever serious?" She waited, then, "No answer?"

"I am trying to think up a masterful non sequitur."

"No—really—don't you ever get tired of strife and war?"

"It doesn't matter. I'm forced to do what I do."

"What do you mean?"

"Somebody has to be responsible for maintenance of the Malthusian Theory. If pestilence, famine, and war had not done their part, the world would have been frightfully overpopulated ages ago."

"I give up," she sighed. "So much for cultivating a serious intellectual conversation."

"I'll get to your intellect by and by. I don't read 'The Playboy Philosophy' until I've looked at the pictures."

"So now I'm a sexual plaything, you pig!"

"That street runs both ways. It takes two to even compete."

Her voice lost its playful banter. "You are very perceptive. I can't understand why I should be surprised. But it is true; I'm not putting any more into the kitty than you. You possess a certain barbaric simplicity that I think I admire. And there's the rub. That could easily turn into something a helluva lot more serious. I can't afford that in my life, not now. I think maybe I won't see you after today."

He smiled into her searching eyes and said, "In that case, we are back to that annoying habit of yours of wasting time."

"You son-of-a-bitch! You don't have any feelings at all, do you?"

He rolled onto her and covered her mouth with his. She bit his lip. Then she stopped resisting and wrapped her arms and legs around him, squirming so that every square inch of their bodies came into contact.

"Yes," she whispered when their lips parted. "Yes, before time runs out."

They finally managed to have the picnic, eating out of the basket as they drove back to the city. They cut it close, but arrived at the door of the hotel as the last sunlight of the day disappeared.

Elana took his hand and said, "Don't come up. Please say good-bye here."

He smiled and nodded. She gave his hand a squeeze and fled up the stairs at the entrance and disappeared through the glass doors.

He lit a cigarette while deciding where to spend the night. He had given up his hotel suite when he took over training, and now Elana's bed was denied him. He decided to hit up Blair. He had an officer's billet at the airfield on the edge of the city and, anyway, that was where the trainees were to assemble for the mission.

Elana was either showing heretofore hidden talent, or she was improving as a player. That display of sorrow at the parting was done to perfection. She had tried the textbook method of extracting information: hit them during the post coital glow and/or stupor. When that didn't get her anywhere, she started to improvise. The star-crossed lovers straight out of a gothic tearjerker; the love that could never be. He guessed the next step to be separating for several days, giving him time to realize how much he really missed her. Then a well planned, casual encounter in a bar, sink the hook and reel in the flounder.

He was ripped out of his vespers by what sounded like a low flying Phantom F-4. The big black limousine roared past his parked jeep, coming from the direction of the palace. He glimpsed the uniformed driver, but the tinted windows protected the identity of any passengers. Then he saw that the rear unit designation plate was covered by a dirty rag. It hadn't been tied securely and the rush of air had torn one corner loose. As it flapped violently, he saw the gold-embossed crossed batons. He threw the butt away and fired up his engine. Now where could Tashfin's personal vehicle be going in such a hurry? He waited until it got a decent lead, then pushed the accelerator to the floor. The way he ran through the gears, the jeep would probably never be the same. But it was expendable.

On a straight run, it would have been no match. But the narrow streets and sharp turns slowed the black bomb. He got as close as he could with his doused headlights and stuck there. The jeep protested loudly at each corner. He hoped that the limo's windows were buttoned so the air-conditioner would mask the pursuit sounds. If the curfew hadn't kept the streets deserted, he would have been an ace inside of ten minutes.

In that ten minutes, he got the drift of where they were headed. The river, which bisected the city, could only be crossed by three bridges, and they weren't near any of them. If the limo kept its course, it would be stopped soon by the waterfront.

And it was. The brake lights ahead flickered, then disappeared to the right between two warehouses. The alley probably dead-ended at the river pier. He pulled into an alley to the left and parked his jeep in the shadows. A second after he cut his engine, he heard the throaty rumble of the limo's engine die.

He covered the distance to the target alley quickly and silently on the rubber soles of his jungle boots. He put his left eye around the corner. He could barely make out the shape of the car parked at the edge of the wooden pier. The driver got out and opened the passenger door. Only one figure joined him. They walked to the front of the car and stood gazing out over the water.

Crates, barrels, assorted bales and litter lined the walls of the warehouse. Chatham worked his way forward, careful not to disturb any loose trash. He got within ten feet of the car, found himself a niche behind a heavy machinery crate, and pulled himself into it. The darkness was like a heavy blanket. He could only make out the shapes of the two men when they moved. He could hear the scrape and shuffle of their feet, but their voices reached him indistinctly.

The driver lit a cigarette. In the flare of the match, Chatham saw the profile of Col. Faran. Either Faran had really screwed up and had been demoted, or tonight's drive was too important to entrust to anyone else. Something about the passenger nagged at Chatham. It couldn't be Tashfin. The figure was much too small.

Both men froze and Faran flipped the cigarette into the river. Then Chatham heard the sound, too.

A muted rumble carrying across the dark waters. Faran walked to the car and reached through the open window, blinking the headlights once. The unseen boat's throttle pushed forward a notch. The boat approached and the pier was bathed in a brilliant spotlight beam.

Chatham kept his eyes on the passenger but his face was still hidden. Immediately, however, he turned his head in reflex to avoid the blinding light. His physical appearance hadn't changed. He was still a dried-up little monkey of a man. And he didn't look much better in the dark suit and tie than in the half-tanned hides and nauseating medicine pouches. But Hamuraba was keeping better company than at the first meeting.

The light winked out and the army motor launch cut its engines and nudged up to the pier, crewmen deftly handling the bumpers. Hamuraba spoke a few words in parting to Faran, then nimbly hopped aboard the deck of the high-speed boat. In the cockpit, the captain waited until the boat drifted away from the landing then opened the throttles and headed north up the river. Without running lights, the launch disappeared long before its echo left the riverfront.

Faran returned to the car. He backed it carefully out of the alley and sped off.

Chatham came out of hiding and paced to the edge of the pier. But there was no clue there to help him.

Riddle: Why should an Mpeche witchman, whose avocation was stirring up the rebels for

Mhlangana, sit down in a cozy tête-à-tête with the Field Marshal? And why would the lion of Ma'ribassa, instead of putting him against the wall, send him back upriver to his brethren in a government motor launch? Chatham hoped that Blair was at the airfield. He supposed he had best get some sleep while he was able.

CHAPTER SIX

The earth is a nursery in which men and
women play at being heroes and heroines,
saints and sinners; but they are dragged
down from their fool's paradise by their
bodies. . . .

G. B. Shaw, *Arms and the Man*

He shifted his weight in the canvas bucket seat
and looked out the view port. The slanting rays of
the morning sun gave a golden wash to the rust
brown and deep green jungle below. The whirlwind's turboshaft engine throbbed, chewing
through the damp air. The ground mist and fog had
burnt away, but nightfall would bring it back in
force.

The engine's vibration was transmitted to the ten
troopers through the thin-walled fuselage. The
quarters were a little cramped, even though the
chopper was designed for fully equipped soldiers.
Chatham had probably overloaded the Zakariyan
officers at that. But, no matter what he had told

them, this was just another training exercise and he didn't expect any contact with the enemy. If he had, they wouldn't be carrying fifty pounds of equipment. By craning his neck, he could see the other ten choppers strung out behind. Blair was with the second squad in the chopper directly behind.

Chatham had assigned one Zakariyan as leader of each squad. He had tried to pick the best of his ragtag company to fill these slots. Squad Leader Mahadi rode with Chatham. He was a treacherous, vindictive weasel, but he was also a fairly decent soldier when pushed into it.

The chopper started to lose altitude, dropping toward the LZ hacked out of the jungle. Chatham pulled open the door before the chopper touched down. As the wheels thumped into the turf, Mahadi had his squad awkwardly tumbling out, one after the other. Chatham gave the interior a final once-over, then followed. The copilot waved from the cockpit and the lightened chopper lifted off. Mahadi was already positioning his men in a defensive perimeter around the edge of the LZ.

In quick succession, the remaining choppers moved in to drop their men and make·room for the next. Blair joined Chatham to observe the simple manuever. The other squads didn't perform with half of the efficiency of Mahadi's.

The other helicopters, to speed things up, did not actually touch down but hovered about four feet above the grass without cutting power. Some of the trainees hesitated in the hatches, weak-kneed, until the press of those behind spit them out. Usually three or four men tumbled onto the unlucky front man. Blair covered his eyes and refused to watch the Keystone Commandos.

Chatham held up the last chopper and loaded on a few of the LZ casualties that would only hold up the march. He weeded out all of the fakers and sent them sternly back to their squads.

When the choppers were gone, he assembled the bloodied survivors. He had 106 less-than-enthusiastic guerrilla fighters.

"All right, listen up," he ordered. "We're behind schedule, so I'll only go through it once."

Most of his tiger-striped warriors were fearfully scanning the bush. He, too, was wondering what he was doing there.

"One of the most important talents you will need to survive is compass navigation. If you miss your exfiltration or resupply point by a hundred meters, it could be the death of you." He stopped to let that sink in. "God knows, Training Officer Blair and I have tried to pound compass reading into your heads. Now is your chance to see if any of it stuck. You will each take turns as pacers and navigators."

"I will admit, gentlemen, right from the start, that I don't have an overabundance of faith in your expertise. In consequence, our first checkpoint will be a two-mile section of railroad track. That ought to be a big enough target for even you. In the second leg from there, we will form up a skirmish line and sweep north along the track. In our path is a village, reportedly deserted. But rebels may have infiltrated so keep alert. A company of the Third Regiment have set up an ambush beyond the village to catch anyone that you may flush.

"Training Officer Blair will accompany the point squad to insure that, in your zealous high spirits, you don't let off a few rounds when you make contact. If you do, the mercs will chew you to pieces. I'll bring up the rear to rescue any babes that get lost in the woods.

"So much for the locker room peptalk. Squad leaders report to Training Officer Blair for your assignments. Check your equipment. We move out in ten minutes."

Chatham wasn't disappointed in his predictions. They almost missed the track altogether, finally making contact a mile south of their target. They left a trail of equipment that the candidates chucked the minute they were out of Chatham's sight. Most of it was ammunition and rations, but some idiots threw away their second canteens. When Chatham drew up his motley command on the track, he kept his mouth shut. Blair later told him that his knuckles turned white on his Sterling. He swore to himself that if some officers fell out with heat stroke, he'd let them lie where they fell. Mahadi's squad was the only one with some semblance of discipline remaining after the morning's trek. He gave them all fifteen minutes for the noon meal.

They formed up again with their skirmish line straddling the track and moved north. Those forced to battle through the jungle on either side cursed their luckier comrades in the thinner growth bordering the track, not thinking that in an ambush the lucky ones would probably be the first to die. Some even moved right up onto the track until Chatham chased them off. Never move on likely routes. Don't walk on game trails, walk beside them. Don't cross streams at fords or bridges, wade across up or down stream. They hadn't listened at the survival classes.

When they reached the village, they halted again to allow the stragglers, just about half of the candidates, to dribble in. There wasn't much left to call a village. There were only three huts with roofs remaining, and they were riddled with gaping holes. Mud walls were crumbling and wood was black and charred from long dead fires. Chatham instructed the troops to search for rebels and caches amid the ruins.

They started out in well coordinated move-and-cover leapfrog. It disintegrated from there on. The first men blundered into the booby traps set by a detachment of the mercs the night before, on Chatham's orders. When the harmless gunpowder charges went off, the nearest candidates opened up with their assault rifles, full automatic, firing blindly into the surrounding brush. Blair and Chatham managed to restore order when they stopped to reload. But in that short time, two men were wounded, one seriously with a sucking chest wound and one had given himself a concussion when he ran into a collapsed roof beam.

Chatham gave up. He divided Mahadi's squad

into point and side security men for protection. The rest he formed into an undisciplined herd, bearing the wounded. He contacted the mercs by wireless and told them they were coming in, to have medics ready and water for those who had thrown theirs away.

And so they came limping in to make contact.

The rendezvous was the depot where Chatham had caught Mahadi's train for the capital. The mercs had set up their camp to the north of the building and, to lessen friction, Chatham had the candidates set up on the south side. They set up a security perimeter like the mercs. But by nightfall, most of them had filtered into the depot faster than Blair or Chatham could boot their asses out. The training officers finally gave up. Blair moved out to try to keep the guards at their posts, while Chatham walked to the mercenary encampment.

He greeted the paras he knew. A few remarks about his candidates were thrown his way, but they withered on the vine when they got a look at his face. What they said was true enough. What bent him out of shape was the fact that he was shackled to the bastards.

"Colonel Chatham. You are with us again."

"The pleasure, believe me, is all mine, Colonel von Heydeck."

They shook hands. Salutes were dispensed within the bush. No sense in pointing officers out to any lurking snipers.

"I am just making my rounds. Perhaps you would care to accompany me?"

"Fine. It will do my soul good to see a little professionalism, for a change."

"I wouldn't be discouraged. Rome wasn't built in a day."

"True. But today is graduation day."

Von Heydeck raised his eyebrows in answer. They moved toward the jungle leaving the camp behind.

"I am sorry to have to bring you the bad news. I am afraid your old LRRP squad has fallen on hard times."

"Did Framere kill them off, too?"

"On the contrary. It wasn't his fault. In fact, after they were trapped, it was due to his clear thinking that L'Escaut and one other got out alive. We recovered most of the parts of the bodies. It seems, in the final diagnosis, Framere wasn't so inept."

They were well into the bush. Chatham glanced around and said, "Where are your perimeter guards."

"It is safe to talk here. There is a listening post about a hundred meters out. It looks like you had trouble earlier."

"Yes. I knew those kiddies weren't ready for the mission. I doubt if they ever will be. But I needed an excuse to make contact with you, so I had to bring them along."

They sat against a fallen tree trunk. "I'll make this fast, then we can get on with the inspection. I still don't know how I will complete the primary. But time is running out. If we don't take action soon, the opposition might.

"If I don't see my way clear soon, I'll have to start risking some long shots, and it will turn into a regular smash-and-grab. Either way, you've got to be ready to jump off the minute that you get my signal. Keep one radio manned at all hours monitoring fifteen hundred kilocycles, both voice and Morse. The code words will be 'Red Wings.' Acknowledge and counter with 'Black Ribbon.' When the sign comes through, get the regiment to the capital and occupy it. You've got some choppers at Sabre One, haven't you?"

"Yes, four."

"All right. The airfield is lightly held, most of the guards on the perimeter. I'd take the four choppers in and use them to invest the field. Send more choppers back, at gunpoint if necessary. And get the shock troops for the rest of the city. In the meantime, you can try to get the bulk of the third in by rail."

"I also have an armored unit at Sabre. I will dispatch tanks with as many troops as they can carry when the first helicopters depart."

"Good. If I can, I will try to disrupt the locals. I don't think you have to worry about the Imperial troops. If the second resists, there could be a real brawl, though. Maybe, when I make the hit, they'll sit in the grandstand until the situation stabilizes."

"All right, from this moment on, consider the third on full alert. I don't suppose I need remind you of the importance of being positive of results before sending the code sign. Many German officers died in 1944 because Hitler's would-be assassin made such a mistake."

"Yes, but he was an amateur."

A burst of fire ripped out of the inky darkness from the direction of the perimeter. Von Heydeck and Chatham flopped behind the log, Chatham charging his machine pistol and von Heydeck drawing his belt gun. Again automatic fire erupted, but of a different cyclic rate.

"AK forty-sevens," Chatham said and von Heydeck confirmed. "Somebody out there just graduated from bows and arrows."

All hell broke loose, muzzle blasts exploding all around them. Most of the slugs whispering through the night air seemed to be coming from the camp. In fact, the firing from out front had diminished to a few sporadic shots. The German and American started their retreat.

When they got near the clearing, von Heydeck yelled the password. It was acknowledged by the countersign and they moved to the tree line. There they found most of the mercs, belly down, facing the depot. A fusillade belched from the ruins and they joined the rest in the dirt.

"What's going on?" von Heydeck shouted to an NCO over the din of the gunfire.

"We all heard the first shots from the LP," the sergeant answered hotly. "We were just about to take cover, when those fuckers in the depot started shooting at anything that moved! They downed some men, but most of the company made it to the trees!"

"Round up some men to probe the perimeter. See what's out there. Radio Sabre for reinforcements. Those remaining, dig in and keep your heads down."

"Fuck that! Let's blow those niggers in the building away first!"

"You have your orders, Sergeant!" von Heydeck's voice was icy.

"Yessir!" the NCO said, without hesitation, and scuttled out of sight.

"I've got to try to stop them quick, or the mercs will, orders or no," Chatham shouted. "Do what you can here. I'll try to circle the depot."

Von Heydeck acknowledged as Chatham headed to the right, following the tree line. Random slugs kicked up all about him like angry wasps as he ran, bent almost double. He swung west away from the track, following the edge of the clearing where the fire wasn't so heavy.

He paused to catch his breath opposite the veranda. Muzzle flashes lit up the windows along the north wall. If he could make it to the door without getting offed, he might be recognized in time.

He lunged out of the cover and ran for the building, zigzagging. His legs jarred his body as they struck the uneven, packed earth. He got halfway and began to think he might actually make it.

Then the beam of a flashlight stabbed out of the structure, catching and holding him. He jolted to a stop to make recognition easier. Somebody dropped the light and he dived to the left. He felt the sonic boom as the rifle bullet whipped by his head.

He lay there in silence, realizing that it had been the final shot.

"It's all right now, Colonel!" Blair yelled from

the doorway. "I've got them stopped, but get in here quick before something else spooks them!"

He scrambled to his feet and loped to the door. He brushed past Mahadi, FN rifle in one hand and flashlight in the other. He shot Chatham's steady gaze back at him, until he turned his attention to the others.

The building was filled with Zakariyan officers clustered around the windows. Shell casings were littered all about, along with empty magazines. Chatham could almost feel the heat from blistering rifle barrels. Powder smoke hung thick in the clammy night air.

"What a bunch of puking heroes," he sneered. "Shooting bogeymen in the dark like a bunch of bare-assed fucking Mpeche. Well, you've accounted for your share of mercs out there. I should let them come in and get you."

He had recovered most of his breath now. "All of you, stay in here. You wander outside and you'll be dead meat. Your biggest danger at this moment isn't from the rebels." He motioned to Blair and started out.

He turned back at the door. "And any man who fires another shot without my express order, I'll skin and gut like a rabbit!"

Blair and Chatham made their way past the medics who were looking to the casualties.

"I was on the south perimeter when the shooting started. I got back as fast as I could," Blair explained. "I tried to order those idiots to cease fire but they wouldn't listen. I had to kick half the asses in there before I got them under control."

"And the last shot was Mahadi's." It wasn't a question.

"Yeah. I saw him at the door with the torch. I could see you out the window, but he must not have recognized you. I saw him start to draw a bead, so I knocked the light out of his hand. He got a shot off, anyway."

A merc came out of the darkness with a flash. "Colonel Chatham? Colonel von Heydeck would like to speak with you. At the LP, sir."

"Give me the light," he said and turned it on Blair's side. "What's this?" There was a small stain above his web belt.

"A scratch. I think I got it while kicking the wogs around."

"Wrong. Look at the hole in your shirt. Mahadi's luck was bad. He missed both of us tonight."

Blair's face got hard. He turned back.

"Relax, Blair. He'll get his. Just keep him in front of you from now on. Okay?"

"Yeah, all right." Reluctantly, Blair stopped.

"Go back and babysit. If it looks like more trouble brewing, get some of the cooler mercs and take away the officers' rifles." Chatham turned to the runner. "Let's go."

They moved through the brush. Not many paras were visible, having fanned out and gone to ground. They came on the listening post, just a wide firing pit with a field phone.

Von Heydeck stood over two bodies stretched out beside it. A medic was working on one of them.

Two other paras flanked the pit, scanning the brush with their rifles at the ready.

Von Heydeck noticed Chatham and came over. His voice was held low to keep from carrying.

"The point men blundered right into the LP. The sentries got the first, but the second put a point-blank burst into the pit. With this."

He handed Chatham the assault rifle. He hefted the squat, ten and a half pound AK-47.

"Probably a Chinese type fifty-six," offered.

"Trouble ahead, Erik. Poison arrows don't worry me anymore."

"I know. Does your sentry know how many there were?"

"No. When the firing started, they pulled back and terminated contact. Didn't even try to recover the points' weapons. The wounded sentry said he saw a lot of bodies running back into the jungle. The dead blacks are over there. Like walking scrap heaps with all the ammo bandoliers and grenades. They weren't carrying food or water."

"Going somewhere in a hurry, in force. And they didn't want to be delayed by a few unexpected mercs that would have been easy pickings. And with weapons enough not to worry about the loss."

"I've got a patrol out after them"

"Might as well save your time."

"Granted. I'm just not taking any more chances. It's a new game with new rules. What happened at the depot?"

"Our allies have a bad case of itchy fingers. Started chopping up the countryside at the first shot.

They downed a half dozen of your men. I'm going to order in the helicopters ASAP. I'll keep them away from your men until the choppers get here."

"Good idea. I have much to do at Sabre. I will say farewell here. Good luck."

"I'll need it. It's going to be a sprint to the wire from here."

They got back to the airfield at daybreak. Chatham supervised the Zakariyans as they turned in their weapons to a makeshift arms room and got them into the barracks with orders to stay there. He completed a written report on the mission with special emphasis on details of the night attack. He sent Blair into the city to hand deliver it to Col. Khalifa.

He guessed the rebel force was headed for the capital. They had detoured around Sabre, and Lamapur was the only other likely target. There was nothing to stand in its way. The only unknowns were its size and speed of travel.

He got a meal and saw to it that rations were delivered to the Zakariyans, then finally fell into Blair's bunk for some rest.

It was dark when he woke. Blair wasn't back. His news probably hit like a bombshell. He had probably been drafted to reinforce the palace.

Chatham's watch read 10:15. He got into a fresh uniform, not bothering to shave or wash. He could stand his own stink a while longer. He wanted to check the barracks first. He buckled on his pistol and walked into the cool evening.

The quarters allotted the candidates were away

from the main hangars and revetments, near the headquarters and control tower. Parked outside the HQ were several jeeps and a Saracen armored personnel carrier, probably for airfield security. Through the open orderly room door he could see the sergeant of the guard and two paras in conversation over a pot of coffee.

He put his head in. "Hear anything about unusual contact with the rebels?"

"No, sir," the sergeant responded, getting to his feet. Chatham motioned all of them back into their chairs. "I heard some rumors about the wogs having automatic weapons. Expecting trouble?"

"I don't know. But I think things are going to get hotter for somebody. I'm at the BOQ. Send a Charge of Quarters runner over if you hear anything."

"Will do, sir."

Chatham continued toward the barracks but never got there. He faintly heard the crackle of small arms coming from the city. Then he heard blasts that were either grenades or antitank rockets. The noise intensified. He ran back to the guardroom.

The sergeant was listening to the field phone as Chatham entered. He barked a yessir and hung up, lunging for his pistol belt hanging on the wall.

"What's been hit? The Palace?"

"No sir. Initial reports say the attack is isolated in the center of the city."

"That's near the International, isn't it?"

"That's right, sir. Nobody knows for sure what they're after. They've set up barricades and ambushes on the main roads leading to the square. They've already knocked out some tanks. Nobody can raise the command post at the hotel. Excuse me, I've got to double security in case they hit here," he said on his way to the door, followed by his CQ runner and the other man.

"Corporal," Chatham stopped them. "Are you the driver of that Saracen?"

"Yes, sir. I've got to load up the guards for the posts."

"I need you more." Chatham cut off the attempted protest of the sergeant. "I'm pulling rank, sergeant. I'll take responsibility. Get your men to their posts some other way."

The sergeant clamped his lip shut and stalked out.

"What's on your mind, sir?"

Chatham turned back to the corporal. "I'm taking reinforcements to the hotel."

"Reinforcements? That APC only holds ten men. And how can we get through? They're punching out tanks."

"The rebels will expect counterattacks from the city. They'll expect the airfield to button up and sit tight."

"And they're right," he interjected.

"I've got some Zakariyans. We should be able to find an unblocked street and go in quick. If we make it to the hotel, we should be able to hold until a breakthrough."

"With Zakariyans?"

"That's my problem, Corporal. Yours is getting

us there. You know where the barracks are?" He nodded. "Next to it is the arms room. I'll meet you there."

Chatham took the barracks' steps two at a time, threw open the door and almost ran Mahadi down. Most of the officers were crowded around the open windows listening to the gunfire and gabbling nervously.

"What is going on?" Mahadi asked.

Chatham ignored him. "I want Mahadi's rifle squad to form up immediately out front. Web gear and ammo pouches only. There's an attack on the Hotel International and we're going in. The rest of you remain here until further ordered. Move it!"

They dragged their heels but were assembled five minutes later. Chatham ticked them off mentally, then moved to the arms room with them in tow. The Saracen was there, hatches and ports open. The corporal was by the rear hatch.

The fat Zakariyan supply sergeant who had checked in their weapons earlier sat shuffling papers at his desk. He made a show of being engrossed in his paper work but winced slightly each time the breeze carried in the sounds of the distant fire fight.

"Open up the arms room."

The fat one looked up quickly, his eyes taking in all of them, then sliding off to a neutral corner of the room.

"I have had no authorization," he complained.

"I just gave it to you."

"But I am responsible. I cannot—"

Chatham moved forward, catching him under both chins, throwing his weight across the desk. Chatham's hand locked on his throat forced him back out of his swivel chair and slammed him against steel bookshelves. Looseleaf regulation binders and supply forms cascaded onto the floor.

"The keys. Or I'll batter the door in with your face."

He made gagging sounds as Chatham's grip tightened, but he fumbled in his pocket and handed over a full key ring. Chatham tossed them over his shoulder to Mahadi, then dumped the sergeant on the mound of multicolored paper.

Mahadi had slipped the padlock off the steel screen door. Chatham slid it back, took the keys and unlocked three racks. He tossed Mahadi and the next man two Sterlings. He pointed out the ammo and grenade crates. He told the rest to take assault rifles from the second rack. He moved to the third and took a Remington 870R riot shotgun with an 18″ barrel. He loaded the extended magazine tube to capacity with seven 00 buck, after pumping one in the chamber. Chatham filled his pockets with extra magnum shells. As he herded the men out, he saw the sergeant still perched on his paper work, afraid to move.

He entered the Saracen first and seated himself in the commander's turret behind the .30-caliber Browning MG. Mahadi took the radio operator's place and the rest crammed themselves into the bucket seats, shoulder to shoulder. The driver closed the rear hatch and clambered onto the bonnet, entering his compartment through the forward hatch.

"Use the back streets, but get us to the hotel as fast as you can. The small arms fire will be no bother. I don't think they have heavy MG's. There's the chance they have PB-forty rockets."

"That will open us up like a tin of beef, sir."

"I know. I'll keep a lookout and hose down anything I can with this thirty. If it gets hairy, we'll bail out and hoof it. Once you get us there, you're on your own to get back to the field."

"Right, Colonel. The meter's running."

The run to the river in the six-wheeler was clean, but they were buttoned up against snipers anyway. Sealed away from the night, the atmosphere was heated by the Rolls Royce engine and soured by the packed, anxious men.

They crossed one of the bridges without opposition. The rebel force couldn't have been too big. The first thing Chatham would have done, given enough men, was take and hold the bridges to protect his entire flank with the river.

Their speed slowed down as the driver started to thread his way down deserted back streets. At times they were so narrow that the sides of the APC scraped ancient stone walls. Chatham kept the turret faced forward, scanning the way ahead.

By his reckoning, they were still a mile from target when they drew fire. The rifle slugs rattled off the lightly armored sides like hailstones. Chatham saw fleeting shapes in second-story windows and chased them with bursts from the light machine gun.

He didn't see any sign of the shoulder-fired Communist rockets. He hoped they had them set up at the opposite approaches. The driver moved steadily forward.

They closed to within a block of the hotel from the opposite side of the square, when the vehicle lurched to a standstill.

"What happened?" he shouted to the corporal.

"Must have hung up on a barricade. It's so dark, I couldn't see. I can rock us off it, but I don't think I can get past it."

"All right, Corporal. Thanks. We'll thumb the rest of the way."

Muzzle flashes from the second floor to the left lit the street. Chatham swung the turret and opened up on a window, splintering the frame. A dark shadow pitched through the opening and landed on the cobbles like a sack of sand.

Chatham squirmed out of the turret, grabbed the riot gun and crawled over the laps to the rear. Pale, noncommital faces stared straight ahead. He unlatched the locking lugs on the hatch and swung the heavy plate open. He stepped to the street.

Jacketed slugs ricocheted off the door from ground level to the right.

He swing around the hatch and zeroed in on the figure kneeling in the doorway. He fired from the hip, the magnum loads rocking him back on his heels. The black slammed into the door, then rebounded face down into the street. Chatham ran, leaping over the corpse. He kicked the door in with a well-aimed boot.

It was a narrow, unlit hall. In the shadows, another figure loomed up. He flattened heavily against the left wall as a stream of hot steel cut the air about three inches from his belt buckle. The AK-47's muzzle climbed up and to the left on full auto before the gunman could jerk the rifle back down on target. Chatham centered himself in the hall and squeezed the trigger. The trench gun bucked viciously in his hands and, in the confines of the wood and plaster alley, the muzzle flash was blinding, the roar deafening. The large shot tore into the Mpeche's chest, turning his guts to trout food.

He stepped over the corpse and kicked open a door to his left. Three naked Arab women cowered in the kitchen, keening, not even aware of his presence. It seemed the rebel liberators had had a little time for diversion.

Chatham heard a footfall on the floor above his head. He flung open the door on the opposite side of the hall: the stairwell.

He bulled forward, taking steps three at a time hoping that speed would overcome the lack of surprise. It was the speed that saved him. As his head came even with the floor, he missed a step, tripped, and pitched forward.

The black had been peering out of the open window, snapping shots at the APC. When Chatham started to clatter up the stairs, he whirled and fired a single shot. It tore into the whitewashed plaster where Chatham's head would have been, but Chatham had dropped to his side, his left arm pinned under him. Lining up the barrel of the gun with one hand and firing on reflex alone, Chatham took the full punishment of the gruesome weapon in his right hand, wrapped around the pistol grip. His wrist was numb, but the black was in tatters crumpled against the far wall.

Chatham scanned the room but there were no other doors. It pleased him no end. He disliked street fighting even more than jungle games. He gladly left the house and the smell of death.

The APC was still there but no sign of his warriors. They were all there, still in their seats, weapons gripped tightly between their knees.

"If they bring up the RB-forties, your cozy little nest is going to get mighty hot," Chatham warned evenly.

They looked at one another, then started to scramble over each other to get out.

"Over there, against the right wall!" Chatham ordered. "Okay, take off!" Chatham shouted to the driver and slammed the hatch.

The officers had flattened against the wall like a line-up, eyes rolling in their sockets trying to cover every window at once. Mahadi didn't run like the rest, but still lost no time in joining his countrymen. The personnel carrier roared back down the street and Chatham climbed the barricade and moved to the sound of gunfire.

He cautiously looked around the corner. On the other side of the square, the floodlit equestrian statue and hotel beyond were in plain view. Half a dozen blacks detached themselves from the front of the hotel and lost themselves in the shrubs and flowerbeds surrounding the monument. In and around the guardpost, along with shattered glass from the lobby entrance, were uniformed bodies in assorted postures of death.

He went back to his men. They wouldn't move their backs from the wall, so he faced them to sketch out the situation.

"We've got to get in the hotel—fast. There's no cover in the square. The faster we flush the riflemen out of the bushes around the statue, the safer we'll be. Stay spread out and keep moving. Let's go!"

"You are mad!" The backlighting from the square revealed Mahadi's face twisted in a grimace of fear. And hate.

"It's the only way. If we do it right, they'll be too busy to pick targets." It was a lie, of course.

"It's suicide! You are crazy even to suggest it! And what for? The hotel was no value!"

The others were starting to catch his hysteria.

The blast caught him full in the chest. The effects of the riot gun are horribly impressive. The officers stared at his remains where they had been tossed by the lead pellets. By the time they remembered Chatham, he was ready.

He held the fragmentation grenade in his left hand, gripping the safety spoon. He held up the safety pin for them to see before throwing it away in the darkness.

"You've got a choice. If you don't move now, I'll blow your worthless carcasses to bloody bits. Your odds are better out there."

They gripped their weapons, then decided that Chatham had made a valid point and started to inch their way to the corner. Once there, they stopped again.

"I'll be behind you all the way. You'd better pray to God I don't trip."

The first man hesitatingly extended his head around the corner. Before the rebels could respond, Chatham shouted go and the first took off like a startled rabbit with the rest on his heels.

Naturally, they forgot all Chatham had told them about bunching up. Erratic fire licked out of the shrubbery and the first two of the squad folded up. Chatham took a grenade pin from his pocket and secured the firing mechanism. He wasn't about to carry an armed frag while playing run, dodge, and jump on slippery cobblestones.

He rehooked the frag to his harness and broke cover, paralleling the thundering herd. He doubted if they would reach the center of the square, much less the lobby.

But the odds shifted. From behind the guardpost sandbags, another Chicom assault rifle rattled. This one, however, was firing into the shrubs. One rebel leaped to his feet then sank back lifeless. Some Mpeche returned fire, only to have it harmlessly chew up the bags.

The Zakariyans were scared shitless, but their self-preservation instincts took over and they charged full bore into the bushes. They sprayed the hidden earth in front of their feet as they moved. It was a wonder they didn't blow their toes off. Their sole interest was removing any obstacle to reaching the hotel.

Chatham knelt in the street and picked off two rebels as they were flushed up the steps at the monument base. He tried a snap shot at another disappearing down an alley but only kicked up an empty cloud of brick dust.

The Zakariyans were on the pavement and entering the lobby, so he trotted after. He kept his eye on the center of the square but detected no movement.

He backed into the protecting shadow of the guardpost and, from deeper in, a voice greeted him. "They've cleared out. That was the last of them. Rearguard to cover an orderly retreat, I should think."

Freddy stepped into the light cast from the lobby, an AK-47 cradled casually in his arm.

"I suppose my command passed you in such a hurry that there wasn't much time for pleasantries," Chatham said. "Thanks for the assist. It would have been touch and go without."

"But you would have made it, wouldn't you, old son." It wasn't a question so Chatham didn't answer.

The officers were huddled in corners and behind wrecked lobby furniture, weapons forgotten at their feet. Not a little incredulous, they were nonetheless thankful for coming out of the assault alive.

A parade ground bellow and they snapped out of

it and started obeying Chatham's orders. Like children, all they wanted to do was please so they wouldn't be sent back out into the dark streets. He had them douse the lights, drag bodies into the bar out of fields of fire and reman the entrance post. They were spread thin, but if Freddy was correct, they would have a quiet wait until government units reached them.

He joined Freddy in the bar, perched on a stool amid the litter of broken glass and corpses. A cigarette dangled from his lips, and the rifle was within reach on the polished bar top. He sipped scotch from a highball glass. Chatham didn't know where Freddy found the ice in the shambles.

Chatham tossed his shotgun beside the rifle and sat beside the Englishman, leaning back on his elbows. Freddy raised his glass in salute.

"Let's hear the story, Freddy."

"Ah, from the much vaunted beginning? Well, let us see. First, the merc guards were relieved by a detachment of Tashfin's finest." He acknowledged Chatham's raised eyebrows. "I suppose he can justify it. The red berets to bolster the palace guard and all, during the troubles. But, all said and done, it did come at a rather propitious moment for our black brothers.

"They hit about an hour ago. Made short work of the Imperial troopers. Those that weren't caught and massacred, ran for it. I was in my room on the seventh floor. I heard the ruckus and, after looking out the balcony, decided it was the better part of valor to present a low profile. I could hear the counterattacks beyond the square, but no one got through."

"They were well organized," Chatham said. "No one could punch through, even armor. The hotel was cut off."

"Yes, well, there were only scattered shots from inside." He waved his arm at the room. "I think they just chopped up the bar and lobby for the hell of it."

"What's your guess for the reason for the attack?"

"Nothing military. I suppose it would be worth some publicity to knock off some influential foreigners: diplomats, journalists and the like."

"Is that what they did? Room to room slaughter?"

"Ah, there's a kicker. After the firing died down, I worked my way down the stairs. They hadn't touched the upper floors. I ran into a straggler, smelled like a whiskey factory, he did. After a short discussion, he made me a gift of this," he patted the rifle, "and I went on my way. Our mutual acquaintances were just leaving. I followed them out, then you arrived."

"What floor did you say they got to?"

"Slipped my mind. Picked up my gun on the second, don't you know."

Pieces started to click into place.

Chatham picked up the shotgun, ignored the elevator, and took the stairs with Freddy tailing.

The drunk's body was in the hallway, a neat little .32-caliber hole centered in his forehead. A few heads peeked out of doors but snapped back as they moved on.

Elana's door hung on the splintered frame by one hinge. Chatham stepped in smoothly while Freddy covered. There were overturned tables, smashed lamps, and cushions scattered in the living room.

Near the foot of the bed in the next room lay another interloper. His throat was shot away. Half-hidden by the sheets was a nickel-plated .25-caliber purse gun. "Ruling out luck, Miss Christian was a dangerous little package if she could stop a man with that toy," Chatham mused.

"No blood. She must have gone with them," Freddy said from a closet. "Without bothering to dress for travel, it looks like." Freddy knew his way around as well as Chatham.

"A message," he said, retrieving a sheet of paper centered on the disheveled bed.

"The People's Liberation Army," Chatham read aloud, "has taken as prisoner of war, Elana Christian, journalist of the Western Imperialist conspiracy. She will be held without harm and released if the following conditions are met. First, a delegation of the Mpeche Nation will be admitted to the General Assembly of the United Nations to disclose war crimes committed by the reactionary puppets now illegally in control of this country. Second, one million pounds sterling will be delivered to a designated representative of the Provisional Government, details to follow. And lastly, the following political prisoners will be released from government concentration camps within two weeks' time." He skipped the long double column list and went to the final paragraph. "If these conditions are not met within the two-week period, Miss Christian will be tried and executed as an enemy of the people for aiding and abetting the corrupt, colonial, war-mongering regime that now oppresses the people. It's signed by Comrade General Mpanda Mhlangana."

"Did you see a typewriter as you came in?" he asked Freddy.

Puzzled, Freddy shook his head.

"Neither did I. The ultimatum is typed. The Comrade General knew who he was after and exactly where to find her."

"That is extremely odd," Freddy commented, a frown creasing his face.

"Odder yet, my spook friend, is that Elana was the target at all. Even you would be higher on the list of influential 'prisoners of war.'"

"Unless she has some importance that doesn't meet the eye," he said, watching Freddy's face. He could have saved his time. He glanced in the living room, then closed the door.

"When is Tashfin's next arms shipment due?"

Freddy checked his calendar watch. "It is after midnight. Four days from today at about one o'clock. Why?"

Chatham ignored the question. "Are you still interested in getting a message to Mhlangana?"

"Yes, of course. But what are you getting at?"

"I'm going to get Elana back. I'll drop your message off."

"Why ask me? You're obviously going regardless."

"I need some unofficial help. Considerable unofficial help. I think you and your government are in a position to supply it."

"Of course, Her Majesty's Government does not condone terrorism. Particularly when not in her best interests. Something could be worked out, off the record, to discourage its spread. I'd have to know the details."

"In all that doubletalk, I take it there is a yes."

"Conditionally."

"Let's speed things up. I'll tell you what I need, you tell me the conditions."

In fifteen minutes, they came to an agreement.

Even in uniform and driving the army jeep, Chatham was watched very carefully as he approached the checkpoint at the gate.

It was 0200 before the advance units of the 2nd reached the hotel. The streets had to be cleared of the burnt-out tank bodies before the APC's cautiously continued their advance. A worm growing teeth is unsettling. Chatham commandeered a jeep and drove for the Palace. The streets were once again quiet, punctuated occasionally by an Mpeche sniper's corpse.

Only after he pulled the vehicle to a stop in the center of a searchlight beam, did a merc officer venture out from a MG emplacement.

"Please inform Field Marshal Tashfin that Colonel Chatham requests an audience, Captain."

He didn't seem surprised. After the previous night's events, an unknown officer wanting to roust the most powerful man in the country in the middle of the night wasn't all that startling.

"With all due respect, sir, I think you should return later in the morning."

"Just ring up Colonel Faran and have him relay that I am here concerning Phoenix."

"Please wait by the gate, sir. I'll contact OD."

The captain returned quickly after a hushed conversation over the field phone, his face neutral.

"Please proceed, sir. The other checkpoints have been alerted so you need not stop. Colonel Faran will meet you at the entrance of the south annex."

He sped through the grounds unchallenged and stopped at the indicated entrance. On the roof, he could see figures manning antiaircraft guns. Some bright boy must have foreseen cannibals attacking with a Mig squadron. An ounce of prevention.

He joined Faran at the head of the marble stairs. The aide was hatless and his normally immaculate patent leather hair was in oily disarray. Chatham noted with satisfaction that he had missed one button on his tunic. He was displeased with the hour of the visit. He didn't speak, but scowled and motioned for Chatham to follow. They clacked down the halls, the only travelers.

They didn't go far. It seemed that Faran never got higher than tour guide. He ushered Chatham in at one of the nondescript doors, then disappeared.

Tashfin looked as if he were about to attend a tattoo at Buckingham, in a dress uniform covered with gleaming medals and orders of nobility. All that was lacking for a state funeral dress rehearsal were the flowers.

He gestured with his arm, encompassing the billiard-sized table covered with street maps and the floor-to-ceiling contour maps of the major continents covering the walls. Dark wood panels, colored phones, electronic consoles and display panels completed the decor.

"Impressive, is it not?"

"To some, perhaps."

"Of course! I forgot," he laughed. "The painfully blunt soldier. My congratulations at your daring counterattack. For which I intend to present you with the Ma'ribassan Order of the Lion with swords, for valor."

"Give it to Major Mahadi. Dead heroes are always more palatable to generals."

"Ah yes, Mahadi. I had received reports of his unfortunate death."

The squad members had been at work early, too.

"What an inspiration his heroism will be to his comrades."

"Yes," Tashfin agreed, "Machiavelli would be proud. Later, I will commission a bust to be placed in a prominent niche in High Command Headquarters. And in six months passers-by will have to read the plaque to recall who it commemorates. And you will get your medal. It comes with a substantial stipend."

He moved to the map table. "I don't suppose you are aware of the big picture, having been stranded with your 'forlorn hope'?" He moved several markers.

"No, but let me make a guess. The rebel force, coming from an unknown base with an unknown number of men and an unknown objective, entered the city, time unknown. They only attacked the hotel and conducted a successful holding action. They retreated in an orderly manner and have now disappeared entirely."

"I have discovered another Napoleon!"

"Wellington," Chatham corrected. "He won."

"Whatever. Nevertheless, your assessment is quite accurate."

Chatham took the rebel ultimatum from his blouse and placed it on the table in front of Tashfin. The Field Marshall read it through in silence.

"The objective?" he said, looking up.

"Affirmative."

"You were a friend of the young lady, I believe. I am sorry."

Chatham frowned in fake irritation. "Save the condolences. I'm going after her. And Mhlangana. Phoenix is reborn."

"I am pleased, I won't deny it." *And not surprised either,* Chatham added mentally. "But you were so convinced it couldn't be done."

"It still can't. Not in the way that you were thinking of. I've got a plan. It involves some risk, not only for me, but for you as well. But it will succeed."

"Tell me more."

"No. I know what has to be done and it will work only if strict secrecy is maintained. And I won't take the chance of political interference. Not even from you. The fuck-up in Vietnam could have been won three days after it started, without meddling amateurs. This is one war that will be fought by the generals."

"Do you realize what you are proposing?" he said in amazement. "You would make yourself the supreme commander of the armed forces."

"Just the Second Regiment. For five days, six at the most. Mhlangana will be eliminated and with him, a large part of the rebel force. Take it or leave it."

"You ask me to give you carte blanche, just like that?"

Chatham didn't answer.

"You speak of risks, then still expect me to endorse this plan?"

"It will succeed."

"You guarantee this?"

Chatham smiled. Tashfin's face split and his roaring laugh bounced around the room.

"I will sign a statement to that effect, if you wish."

"But of course. It makes no difference if you break your word. You will be dead."

"Correct."

Tashfin looked deep into Chatham's eyes, then through him. He broke the trance with a shrug of his shoulders.

"I have gambled before to get where I am. I am not above gambling to remain. I will give you the power."

Chatham took another folded sheet of paper from his pocket.

"A list of orders that I want signed by you by

noon. I want no arguments from senior officers."

Tashfin read the page, then took a deep breath. "You do not exaggerate."

"I will return at noon."

"Wasting not a moment, in motion already. Very admirable."

"No, I'm going to sleep. Until noon, then."

and he was in a bare space, twelve by twenty-five. Cardboard boxes and metal drums were scattered around the concrete floor, and the air was full of lubricating oil and cosmoline.

A man perched on a stool at a littered workbench against the rear wall, bathed by a low-hanging fluorescent light. He was hunched over like a gnome, probably working on some infernal machine. He glanced over his shoulder and, seeing Chatham, spun around on the stool. The infernal machine materialized into an enormous submarine sandwich. He held it in both hands, tearing off a large chunk of crusty bread with his strong, white teeth. He spoke around it.

"Lunch. You know how hard it is to find bologna around here?"

"Want to know what goes into it?"

"Please, no!" he said in horror. "It makes me ill just knowing what's in American bologna!"

His appearance surprised Chatham. But then, what is a whiz kid from S & T supposed to look like? A bespectacled, withered, and pasty English don laboring behind locked doors in the Company's secret lab writing chicken-track formulae for the Deputy Director of Science and Technology?

Peter Nichols, a Ph.D from M.I.T., looked like a wildcat oil driller. He carried a good 240 pounds solidly on a 5'10" frame, and was dressed in unmarked fatigues, tan, muscled arms bulging from the rolled-back sleeves. He had a Milwaukee beergut, bristly gray hair escaping from an open collar, and a bushy Hemingway beard. Looking at the face alone, the pug nose and shaved head reminded him of Porky Pig. Chatham doubted if many people passed that observation along to him.

"Speaking of America, you're a Yank too, aren't you? How did an apple-pie-reared, mother-loving youngster like you sign up with this group of international social workers?"

His surprise was genuine. One department of the Company rarely knows what another is up to. Company "military advisors" have even been known to throw lead at each other from different sides of a fire fight. When the Company desk pushers can't decide which side will win, they sometimes back both.

"And have you ever had an orgasm, or are you a lesbian?"

"They tell me, when I'm not working equations, I'm addicted to hackneyed phrases," Nichols apologized. "So let's start with a few facts. Names —yours and why you know mine—the reason that you are here and are you cleared, security-wise."

"I think this will explain all." Tashfin's order was in his hand.

Without looking, Nichols deposited the sandwich behind him on a small piece of waxed paper in the only open space on the bench. He wiped his palms on his pant-legs and accepted the order. He couldn't have scanned the paper for more than a few seconds.

"Colonel Erik!" he said with delight. "After all this time, somebody is actually going to take my toys out to play?"

"That depends. I don't know what your toys are, exactly. Convince me that they're going to be fun."

"Ah, a chance for a convert. Proselyting commenced. You see, hidden in wood, stacked around you, SPIW's: Special Purpose Infantry Weapons. I've got 'em in two forms: M-16's and M-60's. Besides the SPIW's, I've also got some conventional M-14 sniper rifles, M-79 grenade launchers and M-72 LAW's, Light Antitank Weapons."

He raised his hand imperiously. "Before you ask what is so special about my babies, permit me to speed onward." Not expecting objection, he paused politely anyway.

"These weapons employ Salvo Squeezebore. No, Virginia, that is not a new aerosol laundry detergent. The SSB System basically consists of converging tapered rifle barrel—in the weapon itself—and the SSB projectile."

"Setting the tapered barrel aside for the moment," Chatham interrupted, "let's dwell on this SSB projectile. Translated for a thickheaded lifer."

"Well, let's see now." He rolled his eyes up, clutching painfully for words. "The projectile is actually a projectile assembly loaded into a standard cartridge casing. Several subprojectiles comprise one projectile which are reformed by the taper barrel into bullets which . . ."

"Again please. And please speak clearly and distinctly."

"Oh dear. Well, you take these five cone-shaped bullets, stack them atop one another, bond or encapsule them in plastic, and shove them in a cartridge case where the slug ought to go."

"Fine. Proceed."

"The SSB projectile is fired through the tapered barrel. This is an orthodox cylindrically-bored rifle tube, the muzzle end of which merges gradually into a converging taper."

"Okay, I guess. But watch it."

"After the ignition and propulsion of the projectile, the edges of the subprojectiles contact, engage, and seal in the rifling grooves and are imparted a spin like normal bullets. When forced through the taper, the subprojectiles are swaged, positively forcing separation of the adjacent subprojectiles creating separate bullets. These subprojectiles—or bullets if you will—are spin stabilized and imbued with a diametrical dispersion from the separation point to approximately six mils"—he saw Chatham start to interrupt and increased his pace to finish first—"having excellent ranging qualities caused by their sectional area, after separation, which is a mere fraction of their full-bore propulsion area."

"Please. We've discussed this problem before," Chatham pointed out.

"The taper barrel breaks the stacked slugs apart so they leave the barrel one after the other."

"We are making definite progress, Mr. Nichols. At this rate, we'll have you out of the wheelchair and onto crutches by Christmas."

"Take heart, I'm almost done. The conical dispersion path is about one-third degree included angle which, of course, multiplies target area saturation capabilities. Each subprojectile is lethal to a minimum range of four hundred meters, increasing estimated hit probability at least eightfold."

"I think I've got it, but let's try for a condensed, digested version."

"If I must. And I don't believe for one second that you are all that in the dark. You don't have the glassy stare yet."

He pondered the problem, gave several false starts, then said finally, "The Salvo Squeezebore System creates a shotgun effect in any utilizing weapon without sacrificing velocity, range, or stopping power of the standard cartridge."

"A riot gun with the range of a rifle."

"Longer with light and heavy machine guns. And any single subprojectile is lethal. You could imagine the effect of all five high-velocity slugs striking a portion of the human body simultaneously within one hand span."

"Is the normal cyclic rate reduced or barrel-generated heat increased?"

"Not one bit. The machine gun fires just as fast, say four hundred rounds per minute with a .50-caliber, or five-fifty r.p.m. with an M-60, and each round is transformed into five."

Chatham tried to picture the effect, but failed.

"You have a new proselyte. How many weapons do you have?"

"One hundred M-16 rifles, twenty-five M-60 LMG's, ten .50 caliber HMG's, with about twenty thousand rounds of SSB ammunition for each. Plus about twenty-five M-79's and one hundred LAW's. I'd have to check on the grenade shells."

"In a day or so, an officer and a work detail will be here with my written authorization. I'll take thirty M-16's, three M-60's and several M-79's. Give any necessary instructions to the officer. I can't promise the return of the weapons."

"Never mind, never mind. The sooner they're taken off my hands, the sooner I can be carried back to ole' Virginny. And Colonel?"

"Yes?"

"If you get a chance, let me know any suggested improvements or alterations. We aim to please."

Chatham entered Blair's room in the BOQ. He was stretched out on his bunk, arm thrown across his eyes.

"Rough night?"

"Yes, rather," he answered drowsily. "The rebels weren't all that good, but it was pure hell rooting the snipers out of the buildings. Once the paras got back into the swing of it, it wasn't so bad. We've just been shooting spear chuckers in a barrel too long. Caught flatfooted, we were."

"Think you can do better, now that you're prepared?"

He sat up and looked at me blearily. "Bigger and better things you once spoke of?"

"That's right, Sean. I need some things done, fast. When you finish them up, then you can get some sleep."

"Name it. I know where I can get some benzedrine if I have to," he said, lacing up his boots.

"I need about twenty good men. Excellent parachutists, preferredly ex-legionaires. Officers or EM's, makes no difference. You've got the whole Second to choose from. Take this," he handed him another of Tashfin's orders. "Don't worry about channels. Find them and take them."

Chatham glanced at his watch. "It's fourteen hundred hours now. I'd like to have them in hangar eighteen by midnight. Webbing and water bottles. The rest of the equipment will be supplied. Got it?"

"Right. I know where to look for most of them. We'll be there by two thousand hours."

Zero minus thirty-six hours.

The tarry blackness outside the sealed canopy told Squadron Leader Hensley nothing, so he kept his attention focused on the illuminated instrument dials. The first part of the flight had been the toughest. Not so bad coming in low over the sea. But after landfall, the strain of keeping the phantom jet at an altitude of one hundred feet was almost a living beast tearing at his nerves. The low altitude was necessary to avoid radar detection. If Hensley was downed while invading another sovereign nation's airspace, everyone from the PM to the Chief of Staff of the RAF would be covered with the shit from the fan.

He didn't dwell on this. He was too busy glancing from the terrain avoidance Doppler Radar, to compass, to air speed indicator and back again to the radar. He wished he could have brought along a navigator in the rear seat to take some of the pressure off him. But in the interest of secrecy, this request had been denied. As was the assistance of the radar guidance system based back on The Rock, Micramar.

But now, on the second leg of the flight, Squadron Leader Hensley could almost relax in comparison. He had climbed to 3,000 feet and the invisible tree-covered highlands were less threatening. His check of the instruments was almost mechanical. The speeding jet paced the roar of its twin engines, and only the muted rush of the air sounded in the cockpit. It always had a lulling effect on the pilot, but he professionally fought it off with little effort. Besides, this was his second trip in as many days, and although the technical flight plan was intricate, Hensley's considerable experience made it a milk run.

Hensley was largely in the dark about the flights, as reconnaissance pilots usually are. The previous day had started out as usual for the British outpost on the barren isle. The arid little rock, not much more than an atoll, was starkly functional. Most of the space was taken up with the Royal Naval Base, servicing infrequent ships and electronically spying on that corner of the Indian Ocean. The airfield, capable of launching long-range bombers in emergencies, sat baking in the sun, the squadron of tactical fighters sheltered by the quonset shell hangars.

At midday, Hensley was hurriedly called away from his routine administrative duties by a gasping, sweating orderly, requesting his immediate presence in the base commander's office. Once there, facing both the senior RAF and RN officers, he was informed that a priority, top secret, scrambled signal had been received from London.

All Hensley was allowed to know was that he was being asked to volunteer for a sensitive recon mission over an undisclosed friendly nation. He quickly grabbed the chance to escape from the day-to-day boredom of the austere base. He was then given a further briefing and navigational instructions. They revealed the nation to be Ma'ribassa, but nothing more. Not the reason for the mission nor the objective.

Hensley spent the rest of the day impatiently pacing his quarters, trying unsuccessfully to kill time. After nightfall, he dressed in a sanitized flight suit manufactured in Sweden, carrying no personal papers or identification. No proof of origin if there was a mission failure.

He was then driven to the small hangar isolated on the far side of the field. The security men admitted him to the building. He approached the Phantom F-4, ominous in its coat of flat black paint. It carried neither national rondels nor identification numbers. It had been laundered as well as its jockey.

The skeleton flight crew buckled him in and ran through the pre-flight. The tractor towed him onto the tarmac and, after receiving last-minute data from the tower, he lifted off quickly, kicking the jet into the air with the afterburners. He knew there would be no record of the departure or flight plan recorded in the log in Operations.

As with tonight, he had flown low over the

ocean, so low that there was just the barest register on the altimeter. Then, streaking low over the jungle basin, he roughly followed the Kasambi to the northwest. At a point near the rising highlands, Hensley put the warplane into a steep climb, leveling at 20,000.

This was the calculated risk of discovery. The odds were that any radar operators would not be monitoring this wilderness sector. Hensley was monitoring the Imperial Air Force frequency and could overhear any scramble order. Hopefully, he could then drop back beneath the electronic signals and hedge-hop back to the coast before being intercepted. That would be the only chance for survival, since the recon jet carried no armament.

Once at 20,000 he started a coordinated search pattern. It was not the time-consuming search that it appeared. The nose housing was crammed with vertical, panoramic, oblique and forward-looking cameras loaded with conventional, infrared, and heat sensitive films. In addition, the aircraft was equipped with SLAR: Side Looking Airborne Radar, which could scan and record data for a fifty-mile radius. At his altitude, the sound of his passing could not be detected at ground level, yet the mechanical eyes could record amazing detail. Cameras installed in spy satellites could detect a card table in the middle of Siberia, then tell if it was round or square.

Hensley spent forty-five minutes in the search pattern, computer programmed to cover the most land area leaving the fewest blind spots. After this period, he dropped back down to the deck and made an uneventful run back to base.

When he touched down and taxied into the hangar, he was met by the base commander and a lab technician, besides the ground crew. He stood to one side while the crewman unloaded the various film magazines. When they were turned over to the man from the lab, Hensley left for his debriefing and some sleep.

He must have found something, because upon awakening, he had been informed that he was to make another run, this time to photograph a much smaller area. He was headed for those coordinates now.

He consulted the chronometer on the panel and turned on the final heading of his one and only pass. With gentle fingertip pressure on the controls, he maintained his altitude and heading. With visibility zero, he depended entirely on the minute hand and second sweep of the chronometer to tell him when to depress the camera-activating button in the control grip.

The sweep completed the prescribed revolutions, and he thumbed the button. The infrared cameras in the nose began to operate. Also, in a pod slung beneath the fuselage, a special camera not carried on the first flight began to cycle. The shutter was timed precisely with a built-in strobe light. It was so powerful that it lit up the landscape with almost as much light as that of an overcast day. The light lasted only micro-seconds, too fast to be detected by the human eye. But not too fast for the ultra-high-speed film. The camera and strobe cycled three times in a five-second period.

Hensley held the button down for thirty seconds, then released, hoping that he had passed over the piece of real estate he was supposed to. In the darkness, with the jet exhaust hidden, he knew he couldn't be seen. But there was the sonic boom. At 0100 hours, sleepy sentries would probably quake in fear of the night demons until the sun came up.

He turned back on the new heading.

"Now, just so I don't wrap myself around a palm tree," he said aloud into the rubber oxygen mask as he pushed the control lever down.

Zero minus twenty-five hours.

It was 1200. Chatham sat on Blair's bunk absentmindedly munching from a can of C rations. Ham and eggs. Positively the most horrid tasting mixture conceived by man. He was filling out orders, checking off his list as he went. From the logistics angle, running a war is no fun. Some of his signatures were executed more in scrambled eggs than ink.

Blair had the strike force out at a makeshift range, familiarizing them with their new weapons. Chatham had been out earlier with his. Nichols had not boasted. The submachine gun had handled like its conventional brothers. But when he checked the silhouette, what was left of it, he whistled aloud.

He finished the last of the canned shit and the orders at the same time. The can he threw in the trash basket in disgust and the orders he placed in a dispatch case. He was about to take them to the dispatch rider when he heard a pounding on the door.

Chatham opened it and the rider announced, "Sir, at the front gate, a limey to see you. Says his name is Freddy."

"Okay, I'll be right down. Deliver this to HQ."

Chatham got his headgear and side arm. As he came out, the rider was barreling away on his cycle, siren screaming. All Chatham needed was to have him hit a fat merchant on the street, spreading his orders all over downtown Lamapur.

He strolled through the main gate. Parked just outside was a white MGB. From the left-hand driver's seat, Freddy waved and shouted through his toothy grin.

"Erik, old sport! I promised you that ride. Hop in!"

"Listen, Freddy, I'm pretty busy right now and—"

"Nonsense! You promised and I won't take no for an answer."

Chatham shrugged at the guards and they smiled back in commiseration. He climbed in, Freddy flipped the ignition, and they took off with a squeal of Michelins.

He dropped the act. "I've got the photos. They're under your seat."

Chatham pulled out the thick, sealed manilla envelope and held it on his lap.

"When you are out of sight of the airfield, pull over somewhere. I don't want these getting away from me in this mobile wind tunnel of yours."

Freddy pulled off the asphalt under some shade trees. Chatham ripped open the envelope and started to go through the aerials.

"They came in by diplo pouch this morning. Analyst's comments are typed on the back. First six were taken night before last. Those light specks are cooking fires. They only came out on heat-sensitive so they figure they are under heavy tree canopy, or camouflage, or both. The rest were taken early this morning, at a lower altitude. The infrared turned out pretty good, especially the forward-looking. I've also put in some contour maps of that area."

"Okay. Can you get number ten blown up and crop about one inch of the border for me? Get it back to me in, say, three hours?"

"I think so. Erik . . ."

"Yes?"

"I've helped you out quite a bit, haven't I?"

"Let's not play patty-cake at this stage. Spit it out, Freddy. What do you want?"

"I want to go with you."

"Any special reason?"

"Well, after all, I do have a vested interest. And why send a messenger when I can talk with Mhlangana myself?"

"All right. When you bring the photos back. I'll have a pass for you at the gate. What's wrong? You look like you're having second thoughts."

"No, no. It's certainly not that. It's just that I didn't think that you would agree that easily. I am an unknown quantity in your field and—"

"Oh, quite the contrary, Freddy. You didn't think I swallowed that tripe about your national service being confined to the Royal Catering Corps, did you?"

"Well, maybe not, but—"

"Tashfin is very proud of his collection of dossiers, and to some extent rightfully so. Your section on military service is quite detailed. Commissioned in the prestigious First Dragoon Guards. Volunteered for parachute training, then on to the Special Air Service. I happen to know that eighty percent of SAS volunteers are washed out of training. You completed and were posted to the Third Parachute Battalion in Aden.

"In '64, you took part in the Radfan Operations. Part of a ten-man SAS drop zone marking party, you were attacked by about a hundred tribesmen. After your CO was killed, you led the party in cutting its way out. You were mentioned in dispatches and later awarded the MC.

"Looking for new worlds to conquer, you transferred to the Twenty-second SAS regiment in Borneo. Took part in special jungle patrols and managed to kick the shit out of both Sukarno's boys *and* the Irregular Border Terrorists. You picked up your DCM there. True to form, Tashfin seems to have lost track of you when you resigned your commission and joined MI6. I suppose army life got too tame for you."

"Not so, old man. I really do have an ambitious father, you know."

"Have you been checked out on a para-commander?"

"The 'chute? No, not that one. I've been checked out on other precision 'chutes, though."

"All right. After the briefing, get together with Lieutenant Blair and he'll check you out. He's already done it for the rest of the acbat team."

"Done. I'll be back with the photo as soon as I can."

CHAPTER EIGHT

C'est magnifique, mais ce n'est pas la guerre.
General Bosquet

Zero minus thirteen hours.

The DeHavilland Caribou was designed to hold twenty-four fully equipped paras. There were only twenty-three of them. With the individual equipment bags strapped to each man's leg, there was no room to spare. Chatham sat in the canvas seat nearest the closed rear fuselage doors, next to Sergeant Nogaret, the crew chief and jump master.

Chatham had briefed the team at 1600 hours in Hangar 18. The gear lay in heaps on the concrete, nothing having been issued but the weapons. They squatted on the floor, Blair and Freddy in the front rank.

"We're going to make a night HALO drop," he began. "Some of you have made High Altitude, Low Opening jumps. The others have been briefed as fully as possible on procedure.

"Our aircraft will reach the DZ at an altitude of fifteen thousand feet. At that height, the plane won't be noticed by any ground observers. Meteorologists report a bomber's moon, little or no cloud cover.

Some paras quietly translated into French for their comrades.

"We will drop from fifteen thousand and free fall to one thousand. The altimeters on your main 'chute will automatically pop it. Your reserve is, of course, your manual backup. Because of the thick tree canopy, the DZ will be the Kasambi River itself. It will be very visible in the moonlight. We need it, because we can't send in pathfinders first. While in free fall, you will be able to move horizontally to correct any over- or undershooting.

"You'll each have about eighty pounds of equipment in your leg bags. They have been fitted with self-inflating collars that activate when you hit the water. But be prepared for malfunctions. Any questions on the HALO itself?"

He waited for the translations, but there were no questions.

"All right. Now, for the objective."

He moved to the makeshift easel and turned the three-foot-square enlargement around to face the intent paras.

"We are going to hit the rebel base camp, engage and divert their forces until relieved by elements of the Second.

"This aerial recon photo was taken early this morning. The light patch in the center is a roughly circular clearing about one thousand meters in diameter. Intelligence says it is composed of rock and gravel with little concealing brush. There is a gentle incline north to south. On the north fringe is thin tree cover. Camouflage netting and foliage has been woven into the upper branches. Hidden beneath this canopy is the camp. By means of cooking fires, the rebel force is estimated at fifteen hundred, armed with rifles and automatic weapons.

"Bordering the south is a high cliff. This irregular mass at its foot is the ruin of a large stone building, probably an Arab mosque or fortress.

"The DZ is about four miles from the objective. We drop at twenty-four hundred hours. We'll regroup on the west bank and proceed up the foothills, covered by moderate forestation. Rough going, but we should make the clearing by oh-three-hundred hours. We enter from the south and take up position at the base of the cliff to protect the flanks and rear. There should be plenty of cover in the ruin."

"If our strikeforce has not been discovered by dawn, we will engage."

"Some of you are officers. I will be in command and, regardless of seniority, Lieutenant Blair, my XO, will take command in my absence. Your equipment will be issued immediately. You will have ample time to check it out because you are confined to this area until our transport arrives at twenty-one-thirty hours. Good luck to us all, gentlemen."

The loud drone of the twin engines prevented all

but shouted conversation. Most of the men sat, withdrawn, their arms folded over their belly reserve 'chutes. Some smoked, a few dozed. The prejump tenseness hung in the air like static electricity.

Nogaret sat forward and pressed the intercom headphones tighter to his ears. Chatham couldn't hear what he responded into the mike, but he turned to Chatham and shouted, "Five minutes, Colonel."

The plane banked, then leveled off on the final heading. The rhythm of the props changed as the pilot throttled back.

Chatham turned to the quiet paras and yelled, "Stand up, check equipment!"

Each checked the man in front and sounded off when all was in order.

The cargo doors swung open and the roar from the black void invaded the confined interior.

"Stand in the door," he ordered and moved into place at the head of the line.

The men shuffled to the rear, clumsy in their temporary weight gain. They ignored the steel cable running the length of the fuselage. They wouldn't use static lines in free fall. The red glow of the single bulb near the door was the only illumination.

Chatham looked down. The moonlight was swallowed by the jungle and the rising hills to the right. Only the placid river threw the light back as a silver ribbon. It looked clean and pure. But he was a realist from way back.

The red winked out, replaced by the green.

Nogaret slapped Chatham on the butt and yelled go. Chatham shuffled to the end of the ramp and jumped into space.

The prop blast kicked his legs out and stretched him horizontal as he assumed the parachutists' form: arms gripping the reserve, elbows pressed into his sides, legs outstretched, knees and ankles together. When he cleared the turbulence, he rolled over on his belly and spread-eagled his arms and legs to fly.

The plane flew on, leaving cotton wool stillness.

Over his shoulder, he saw the others strung out and suspended above him in the moonlight. In the silence, with the wind flattening his cheeks against the goggles and helmet straps, he felt weightless. But he knew he was falling at terminal velocity into his violent world.

He forced his attention back to the river, fast rushing to meet him. He was off to the left over the crouching trees. He shifted position and planed until he was centered over the band of water again. The darkness ruined his depth perception and even with the luminous dial, it was difficult to read the altimeter. That's why the 'chutes were equipped with automatic releases.

The lower he descended, the faster he seemed to fall. He felt the pop as the primary opened and he prepared for the jolt. When it came, the harness cut into his groin and shoulders. The eighty pounds strapped to his leg didn't help.

He gazed up, reassured by the dark green canopy. He located the steering risers and tugged until he was back on target.

Chatham reached down and popped the quick-release buckles on the equipment pack and mentally flinched again. The bag fell away, momentarily making him feel light as a feather. Then it reached the end of its elasticized webbing tether strap attached to his ankle. After the shock, he tested his leg gingerly. Everything seemed in order. Sometimes the ten-foot length of webbing doesn't give as it is designed to and snaps the leg out of its socket. A midnight swim with one good leg in a jungle river is not something he looked forward to.

He was ready to hit when he saw the half-submerged tree trunk. It was too late to change course, so he tucked himself into the landing position, hoping for the best. He heard the splash of the bag, then he hit.

He went beneath the surface. The first task was to escape from the parachute harness. In the inky solitude, all of the quick-release buckles functioned and he struggled out of the straps. He clawed his way out from under the floating silk and entangling risers. He was attuned to the slightest pressure on his leg. If he felt the tug of the sinking bag, he was ready to slash free with a combat knife before he could be dragged into the choking bottom mud.

He broke the surface and sucked air deeply. He trod water while trying to get oriented. Silhouetted in the moonlight, he saw that the equipment bag was snagged solid to the jagged stump. He swam to it and half pulled himself out of the water.

He unstrapped his helmet and let it slide into the

water. It quickly sank, and he was free of that unnecessary weight. He examined the waterproof bag as best he could in the poor light.

One of the collar floats had been ripped by the rotting wood. The others had inflated properly. The shore was about seventy-five meters away. It would be a long swim, towing the damaged bag. That's if it floated at all.

He unstrapped the tether line and discarded it. He tugged at the bag, but it remained firmly anchored to the stump. He tried to get purchase on the slippery surface, but even the cleats on his hard rubber soles wouldn't catch. He felt with his feet, found an underwater crevice, and wedged his foot in. He grabbed the bag with both hands and tugged until he thought his protesting back muscles would crack. He started to quiver with exhaustion and gave one final heave in desperation.

The rotted wood gave way and the bag with it. He kept his hold and went over backward, the bag clutched to his chest. If he let go, he knew he would lose it in the night. Instead of floating to the surface, the bag bobbed heavily and settled iceberg low. It didn't sink but it was dead weight. He headed for the bank with powerful leg kicks, barely succeeding in pushing the burden in front. Just as he thought he would have to cash in, his feet touched the soupy bottom.

The muck fought to hold his feet, but the bottom was just firm enough so that he could get a shoulder under the bag. He half waded, half fell the rest of the way to the bank.

It was mostly slick mud rising steeply for three or four feet. He gripped the bag in one aching hand and found an exposed root with the other. Somehow, he managed to beach the equipment after a ten-minute struggle and lay gasping beside it on terra firma.

He recovered enough to sit and cut the fastenings on the waterproof material. He pulled out the XM-177E2 submachine gun. That's a hell of a destination code for the chopped-down version of the M-16 with a Sionics silencer clapped on the business end. He fished out a banana clip, inserted it, locked and loaded.

He crouched by the bag and softly whistled a low note. The jungle had fallen silent with the intrusion, and he knew the sound would carry quite a distance. But he didn't think Mhlangana would have patrols out this deep in his own territory. From the north came an answer.

Within twenty minutes, eighteen camouflaged fighters crouched with him.

"Who's missing and why?"

"Last I saw of Sergeant Steiner," answered Blair, "was when he hit the water. He didn't come out. Lieutenant Murat and Corporal Hansen overshot and got hung up in the trees. Murat hurt his back and can't be moved. Hansen just sprained an ankle, but he will slow us down too much. He will stay with Murat until we can medivac them. And Captain Smith is just missing. Nobody saw him come down."

"What about the equipment?"

"Smith didn't have much of importance. An M-60 was with Steiner. Murat and Hansen had some M-60 ammo, an M-79 and some grenades. I threw the machine gun ammo in the river and split the rest among the others."

"All right. We can't spare the time to search for the missing. Get the gear out of the bags and onto the pack boards. Get the points and navigator started up the slope. The rest to follow shortly."

Ideally he would have security surrounding the main force and would have gone slow enough to maintain complete silence. But he had neither the manpower nor the time. The points were armed with silenced weapons to take out anyone they blundered into.

The bush wasn't all that thick because of the altitude and barren soil. But they were climbing the ridges of the foothills and some inclines were fifty degrees. It was rough going for him, and all he carried besides his own weapon, harness, and ammo, was the rifle case strapped to his back. The air was cool but they were seal-slick with sweat five minutes after starting.

Freddy climbed beside Chatham. He was in fairly good shape, but not that good. The last half of the trip he made on willpower alone, knowing that they wouldn't slow up for him.

Two and a half hours after leaving the river, word was passed back from the point that they had reached the plateau. Chatham gave the team a five-minute break and caught up with the point on the rocky lip of the clearing. He lay down between the two paras and accepted the glasses.

He could make out the ruin at an angle to the left. He couldn't see much beyond with any clarity, but there was a lot of flickering light among the trees. Too much light for cooking fires.

He turned his attention to the terrain between them and the stone wreckage. He picked out the characteristics that he remembered from the maps. He handed the binoculars back to the para, instructing him to select the route with the most cover.

He moved back through the men, reminding them to maintain silence from here on. He headed the small column as they worked their way to the goal. Even at the irregular pace—dodging from cover to cover—they were soon into the ruin.

Not much of the rubble was recognizable. A few broken columns, bits and pieces of mosaic and carved blocks. That was all that remained of what? An Arab mosque? A Coptic monastery or even a lost Roman legion's last outpost? If it had been a fortress, it was about to get one last reprieve from oblivion.

What with the noise of the drums and howling voices carried to them on the night breeze, the silent movement had been unnecessary. The men picked their places with an instinct for the best fields of fire. Chatham settled behind a massive block of quarried stone and shrugged out of his equipment harness. Afte checking with each of the men, Blair joined him and offered the glasses.

Resting his elbows on the stone, Chatham systematically scanned the tree line. The light from the fires supplied more than enough illumination for the night lenses.

He could make out figures dancing and jumping between the masking trees, backed by the flames from bonfires. Some party. With a little more difficulty, he spotted the guards scattered haphazardly at the edge of the clearing. Most of them seemed slumped over in a stupor or gazing longingly back at the festivities from which they were excluded.

"See that sentry off to the right?" Chatham handed the glasses to Blair. "Away from the rest? By the large tree?"

Blair moved the glasses in short, choppy arcs, then froze and grunted acknowledgment.

"He looks the least drunk. Send a couple of the men out to get him. Bring him back in more or less one piece. I want to ask him some questions."

Blair moved back to the others. When the two raiders moved past him, he wasn't surprised to see that Blair was one of them.

There was the rattle of pebbles as someone moved next to Chatham. "What are they up to, Colonel?" Freddy asked.

"Getting a prisoner to question."

"What if he doesn't want to talk? Those blacks out there are notoriously closed-mouthed."

"He'll talk, inside of five minutes."

"And what subject will he discuss?"

"The layout of the camp. I'm going to get to Elana, if she's there." Because where she is, he is, Chatham said to himself. "Come morning, that side of the clearing won't be very healthy."

"It's a matter of some discussion as to how safe this side is going to be. Care for some company? For some unexplainable reason, I feel responsible for Elana, poor thing. We are friends, after all."

I'll just bet you are, Chatham thought.

"No. You may be good. But I don't know how good. I can't take the luxury of educated guesses."

"But evidently you're good enough?"

"Damn right you are, Freddy." After that, they sat in silence gazing out over the killing ground.

Long moments passed, then dark shapes rose up before them. This time there were three. Blair and the para supported a limp Mpeche warrior between them.

"I noticed a caved-in cellar of some sort back there," Chatham said to Blair.

"I know the one."

"Take him there."

They moved past, dragging their unconscious captive. Chatham followed them and Freddy followed him. Along the way, Chatham picked up two more men.

Not much was left of the subterranean room. Most of the granite ceiling had caved in, filling the rest of the space with rubble. It left little more than a pit ten by twenty by ten deep, partially roofed. They crowded in. It smelled of dry, dusty catacombs.

"I doubt if he'll yell when I bring him to," Chatham said. "They pride themselves on facing death with stoic silence. But be ready in case we've got a nonconformist."

Blair moved in behind the black.

Chatham had him seated on the floor, his back pressed to a large rock, a para on each arm holding them immobile to the stone. He was covered with animal fat that made his skin glisten through the patches of dirt and paint. The stench was overpowering. Mpeche apply the grease before a war and don't remove it until the fighting's done, just add fresh layers. Instead of a loin cloth, he was rich enough to possess a ragged pair of shorts. His head lolled on his chest and his legs were splayed out in front of him.

"If he thrashes around too much, you two grab his legs," Chatham instructed the new men.

"Surely you're not going to torture him?" The horror in Freddy's voice indicated it just wasn't done on the playing fields of Eton.

"No, I'm not. Because it wouldn't do me any good in the short time I've got. Wake him up."

Blair brought him around with some water from a canteen. Chatham switched on a flash and placed it in a niche so that it shone down on the black, half blinding him. He glared back balefully with no fear in his eyes.

Chatham took a grapefruit-sized rock, knelt between the black's feet and smashed his knee. The Mpeche didn't make a sound but Freddy yelped.

"You said you wouldn't torture him!" he said hotly.

"I'm just getting his attention. Now shut up and stay out of it," Chatham ordered coldly.

He had reasons for the seemingly needless

brutality. By causing the black pain, he brought home to him that he was at his mercy, no limitations. The Mpeche live a harsh and savage life that teaches them to regard compassion with utmost contempt. And lastly, thinking about the omnipresent pain kept his mind busy, making it harder to scheme and lie when questions came. But Chatham wasn't about to explain this all to the Englishman.

The warrior bit his lower lip with teeth filed to points and the blood dribbled down his chin. His neutral expression was unchanged. The ragged breathing was the only other evidence of pain.

Chatham leaned forward, speaking in the dialect. "Is this then the mighty warrior?"

His eyes widened in disbelief of Chatham's knowledge of his tongue.

"No, a weak, blind old woman who can be caught easier than ground snails. I have questions for you, son of the carrion-eaters. You will answer me with the truth."

The Mpeche drew back and spit. Chatham hoped his brothers were no better marksmen. The bloody sputum dribbled from his fatigue blouse.

Chatham sat back on his haunches, drawing his knife from is bootsheath.

"Stretch out his left arm and put the wrist on that flat rock," he ordered in English.

Freddy exploded again. "What are you going to do?" he shouted, moving forward.

Chatham nodded to the two paras beside him. "Shut him up till I'm finished."

They moved like cats, pinning his arms and clapping a hand over his mouth.

The Mpeche is a clansman. A man without a clan is an outcast, the lowest of the low and no Mpeche fears anything more than being declared an outlaw.

One of their customs, like several other tribes, is that the right hand alone is used to clean up after one of the body's functions. The right is unclean and it is taboo to eat with it.

Chatham laid the sharp edge of the blade lightly on the top of the warrior's wrist. He recoiled from it like it was white hot. The paras held him firm.

"You have a simple choice, old woman. Refuse to answer truthfully, and I will cut off your hand. Then your father will hide his face from you and your clan brothers will chase you from the camp with stones. Your soul will wither and die, even though your carcass lives on slugs and worms as you wander alone in the jungle." Now he made no attempt to hide the fear. "I will give you back your hand, pus of an infected dog. Answer."

The black's eyes leapt from face to face. Except for Freddy's, all were set and hard. Chatham put pressure on the blade, and a trickle of blood formed from the cut. A para's calloused hand smothered the scream in the warrior's throat.

"Now, will you answer?"

He nodded his head, and Chatham signaled the merc to let go of his mouth.

"Why is there a celebration tonight?"

"Mpanda, Cat of the Jungle, has returned after a great victory over the colorless ones," he replied with a trace of pride. "With him he brought a trophy, a white woman much valued by the plainsmen. Mpanda himself caused the liquor and bhang to be given out and for tonight he allows us to mate with any woman willing. After his pleasure has been slaked, Mpanda has promised the white bitch to Hamuraba, the greatest wizard. He will make magic with her and we will kill our enemies and live in riches on the plateau."

"Where does Mpanda dwell in your camp?"

"Near the outer edge. We built him a hut in which to rest and mate with the white one."

"The white woman is with him?"

"To service Mpanda's lust whenever he wishes. When he returned, he coupled with her before the tribe to show us his great power."

"And Hamuraba, where is he?"

"I do not know. He is everywhere, never in one place."

"He is not here." Chatham rose and told the paras, "That's all I need. Kill him."

Freddy caught up with him just outside the vault. Chatham turned to confront him.

"Before you stoke up your horror and indignation to a fever pitch, I'll explain it to you. Just once. We take no prisoners. I will not assign one man to guard duty when we are likely to get our asses kicked way out of shape at sunup. Would you have done differently?"

Freddy was silent.

"Think with your head, for once," Chatham advised. "Now there is one thing and one thing only I want from you. I'm going to get Elana out and I don't want any of her unnecessary playacting. Give me her recognition code."

A blank look settled over Freddy's features.

"I've got no time for your pathetic playacting, either," Chatham snapped. "For chrissake, it was plain as the nose on your face from the start that she was your stringer. Any fool could have seen that." Smashing a knee could be figurative as well as actual. "Now I want that code."

"St. George's Cross," he said simply.

"Thank you, Mr. Spy Master," Chatham turned on his heel and left him there.

From the OP, he scanned the camp again. Blair arrived and he told him, "I'm going in. If I get caught, you'll hear about it. They're in no shape to send out probes. Just sit tight till daylight."

"Okay, boss." He flashed a tense grin and put out his hand in the dark. "Thanks . . . for everything," he added as Chatham gripped it.

Chatham took out the Smith and Wesson Model 39 from the butt pack at his feet and made sure the silencer was fitted properly. He pulled back the slide and jacked a 9-mm cartridge into the chamber and set the safety. He attached the Seventrees scabbard to his web belt and dropped the pistol in. He stripped off all of the magazine pouches and put two grenades in his shirt pockets. He checked to see that his knife was still strapped to his leg, then started out.

He eased into the clearing, setting each foot

down slowly toe first, feeling for loose rocks before putting down his full weight. The first five-hundred meters or so were nothing but sharp, uneven rocks so he moved in a crouch. He headed for the vacated sentry post.

When he had covered half the distance, the ground was softer and tufts of coarse grass grew barely knee-high. He slid prone and continued. The breeze moved the grass in dry rustles and concealed his motion. With the tiger suit, camouflaged face and arms, he knew he was nearly invisible.

He was almost to the trees when he froze, hearing a clacking noise that he couldn't place. He kept his head still, searching with his eyes.

Then he saw him. Another sentry squatting on his haunches fifteen feet away, his back to Chatham. Finding his friend gone, he had hunkered down to wait. He rattled pebbles in his hand causing the clacking that had alerted Chatham. A rifle lay carelessly in the dirt at his feet and a *seme* hung in a scabbard tied around his shoulder with a cord.

Chatham placed the knife between his teeth so that it wouldn't brush accidentally against rocks. He edged closer, keeping directly behind the quarry, positioning to strike.

Slash a wrist artery and it takes thirty seconds to lose consciousness and two minutes to bleed to death. Slash the artery on the inner arm at the elbow and it still takes fifteen seconds to pass out. Attack the throat and kidneys, and you've got a thrashing body.

When Chatham could reach out and touch the naked back, he got to one knee. He flung his left forearm around the black's throat to hold the target steady and slammed the point of the knife into his temple. Chatham felt momentary resistance of the thin, brittle bone, then the blade went in like cutting unripe melon. The sentry collapsed on his butt. Chatham removed the blade and lowered the body. He wiped the unseen wetness from his hand and knife on his victim's scraps of clothing, and moved on.

There were many shapes wandering in front of him, and he knew that he would not go undetected if he kept his present course. A little to his right, he saw a looming, dark mound and made for it.

When he got next to it, he recognized it as a large stack of wooden crates of many sizes. The pile was about ten feet high with camouflage netting draped over it. He couldn't see how long it was because the end was lost in the brush. He lifted the netting and crawled under.

The bonfires raging on the far side produced some flickering light even under the net, and only by crouching back against the boxes could he find the shadows he wanted. There was a smaller pile beyond the netting that formed a corridor leading to the party, which seemed to be dying in intensity. From the open crates on the smaller pile and a mound of garbage against it, he guessed that its crates contained canned rations. He was curious about the nature of his refuge.

There were a few crates anchoring the edge of

the netting catching most of the light. They were
stamped with a variety of scripts. He recognized
but couldn't decipher the Chinese and Korean. On
another crate he could make out *ruzheina
moptipna* and on another *Kulometna pistole
munice*. Russian grenade launchers and Czech machine pistol ammo.

He craned his neck to study those against his
back. The stenciling was very faded. Then he
started to make it out. He checked some more
crates. Same thing.

Mrs. Chatham's clumsy son was squatting in the
middle of who knows how many tons of C-4 plastic
explosive, ripped off from the U.S. of A. somewhere
along the line. There wasn't much danger, even
with the drunks and their fires on the other side. It
would take detonating caps or cord to set it off. But
when it was set off. . . .

He stiffened as a shadow danced in the supply
dump corridor. Its owner was making slow
progress, bouncing from wall to wall. He staggered
by Chatham, almost landing in his lap, before regaining his precarious balance. The Mpeche tossed
the bottle on the trash heap and continued to some
bushes where he took a piss that should have been
a contender for the endurance record. He returned
to camp on as straight a line as he could manage.
From the strength of the smell that wafted from the
bushes, it seemed to be a popular latrine.

Chatham climbed to the top of the pile, found a
gap in the netting, and cautiously peered through
to get bearings. Below, the fires sent up columns of

sparks and smoke from dying flames. Ebony bodies were all around, thick as a carpet. The hour was late and very few merrymakers were still on their feet. Most were asleep, some in the arms of their female comrades. Some still attacked bottles half-heartedly. The minute remainder either wandered aimlessly or were aiming for the Fred Astaire Twinkletoes Award.

He was lucky. At the edge of the circle of light, he saw the hastily built hut. If luck held, Mhlangana would be at home with his milk-white steed when he came calling.

He spotted a ditch running through the crowd and coming within ten feet of the rear of the hut. It looked like the best route. He hoped it was deep enough. He wouldn't find out, perching like a parrot. As the Marines say, do you want to live forever?

It took him five minutes to get down and round the far end of the ammo dump. The gulley originated on his side. It must have once been a stream; the bottom was covered with sand and gravel. Where he entered, it was about waist deep with steep sides. The sand silenced his passage so he moved at a steady walk.

He could hear clearly the snores, sleepy groans, and wretching as he went. He mentally gauged his progress. He wasn't about to stick his head up for a look. The sand started to merge with gravel, and he had to slow his pace.

It was good he did or he probably would have stepped right on the lovers. Or lover, singular. From what he could pick up of her drunken complaining, the warrior and his ladyfriend had started prelims on the bank above. Either the pace got out of control or else the bank gave way under the pounding. At any rate, they both ended up in a naked tangle in the middle of the ditch. Her main complaint was that the fall had made him lose interest. It was likelier that he had knocked himself senseless or had passed out. When grinding her loins into his and pushing her greased breasts in his face brought no results, she crouched over his hips, working diligently with both hands.

The knife-edge of Chatham's hand snapped her neck and she died, not knowing the honeymoon was over. He killed the second half before he woke.

Finally, he did hazard a look. He had gone past the hut by several yards. He looked it over from the rim. It was round, about ten feet in diameter with a steeply pitched thatched roof. The walls were made of plaited branches with blotches of mud put on slap-dash. A thin trickle of blue smoke twisted out of the hole in the peak of the roof.

Chatham drew the pistol and snapped the safety off. The next move was chancy. The door faced the crowd. If there was a guard, he would have to eliminate him in full view of anyone who cared to look.

He moved out of his cover and up to the wall. He inched along it, sheltered beneath the low roof overhang. He was now partially in the view of the revelers. His luck still held. There was no guard at the open doorway.

The entrance was barely three feet high. He

dived through, landing on his stomach. Some light made it through the chinks in the wall. But the smoldering coals in the central fire pit generated a smoky haze that filled the room. His eyes smarted, but he could see well enough to recognize the only occupant.

Elana was a pathetic little bundle, bound hand and foot, cowering against the plaited branches. Her face was frozen in a rictus of fear. Recognition began to dawn and her rigid face melted in quiet tears.

Her voice was very low and he almost didn't catch the words.

"He hurt me, Erik. Oh God, he hurt me. Again and again. I lost count. Each time was worse than the one before. . . ."

He moved to her while she droned on. Her naked body was covered with grime, cuts, and welts. Her hair was filthy and matted.

"Then . . . in front of all those animals . . . the shame . . . I'll never be clean again." She lowered her face into the dust.

He knelt and cut the hide thongs. He stood up and said softly, "So what do you want? A medal?" Her body went rigid. "A St. George's Cross?"

The silence was thick and oppressive. Or maybe it was the smoke. She laughed deep in her throat. She sat up, flexed her wrists and tried unsuccessfully to wipe the grime from her face. She only moved it around a little.

"God, I'm sore. How long have you known, you bastard?"

"Since the first." He unbuttoned his fatigue shirt, pulled out the bundle of clothing and handed it over.

She unwrapped it, set the soft leather moccasins to one side and started to pull on the smallest set of green coveralls that he had been able to find at the airfield.

"Where's Mhlangana?"

"The mighty savior is out visiting the clan elders. That could put him anywhere. He's got a hell of a lot of men here, from what I could see." She pulled on the boots, stuffing the too-long coverall legs into the tops.

"Did I say mighty? Before he raped me for his boys, he sat in here and cried in frustration because he couldn't get it up. The son of a bitch is ninety-five percent impotent. He was encouraged by his rare success in the main event and brought me back in here to try for an encore. He almost made it a couple of times, in a half-assed way. Mostly, he just got his kicks by using me as a punching bag. Feels like the bastard caved in my ribs. The trip here was the worst. Even after my feet gave out, and they carried me, it was no picnic." She finished zipping up the clothing.

He put his fingers to her lips and she stopped talking instantly. A shadow fell across the portal and black legs halted square in front. A rifle was propped against the wall and the big tribesman sat in the dirt facing the fires, leaned back and blocked the entrance.

He mouthed Mhlangana's name to Elana but she

shook her head no. She placed her lips against his ear and breathed, "The guard. He must have left just before you arrived."

He moved along the wall toward the guard. He raised the pistol. His head was out of sight. Chatham couldn't risk a head shot anyway. The high-velocity, full-jacketed bullet might go right through and he couldn't guarantee where it would end up.

He lined up the muzzle about three inches from the small of the back. The first round smashed his spine. Quickly, Chatham triggered two more, kidney and lung. His instructor at the Farm had always taught never to use one when you could use two or three. The only noise had been the click of the slide. The mark lifted slightly, gave a low cough ending in a wheeze, then settled again.

There were no shouts of alarm. After a quick look, he took Elana's hand and they made it to the dry streambed safely. Elana was limping. He shortened his stride and she kept up without a whimper.

They passed the two corpses and made the relative security of the dump. He led her to the corridor and pushed her back into the folds of the netting. He handed her the pistol. She checked to see that the safety was off. He turned to his work, secure in the knowledge that anyone blundering on them was in for a world of hurt.

The most time-consuming part was prying up the lid of one of the crates. When it finally came free, he pulled out a one-pound block of C-4. He discarded the wrapping and kneaded the plastic explosive until it was pliable, then set it down and crossed to the trash heap. He took out the roll of fine piano wire that he always carried and tied one end securely to a heavy crate one foot off the ground. He grabbed an empty can and returned to the netting, stringing the wire behind him. He slipped the coil over his left wrist so he wouldn't lose it in the dark and removed a grenade from his pocket. He tore off several thin strips of C-4 and pressed them around the grenade. He wedged the tin can firmly between two crates horizontally and tried the grenade for size. It lay there loosely but the can was tight enough to hold the safety spoon in position. He drew up the slack in the wire and fastened it to the fuse assembly of the frag. He sat a smaller box under the suspended wire and wrapped the remaining C-4 around the filament, resting it on the box so its weight didn't pull the grenade out of its nest prematurely. He removed the safety pin and his booby trap was complete.

Any sharp tug on the wire would pull the grenade free and bury it in the pound of C-4. Once free of the can, the spool would fly off, the striker would hit the detonator and the grenade would go off and explode the plastic with it. How big of a bang depended on how much more C-4 was stacked around. He hoped that the next drunk wouldn't answer the call of nature before Elana and he got well clear of the area.

He took the pistol back and they put some distance between them and the camp, retracing his route.

When they neared the ruin, he stopped and whispered, "Be careful to shadow me. We've got Claymores set out and I don't want you getting tangled up in any detonation wires." He gave the low whistle and led her in when he got the answer.

Blair met them, but Freddy was nowhere in sight.

"See what you can repair with the first aid kit, Sean. Then give her a canteen or two of bath water," Chatham said to her retreating back. Blair grinned and followed.

Hlobane felt uneasy and could not sleep. There were several reasons why he lay near the embers in drugged wakefulness.

The liquor that he had drunk in great gulps had at first animated him. But now it lay in his stomach like a cooking fire charring raw meat. He was sick but he dare not vomit. Then he would be forced into an all-night vigil lest some secret enemy steal part of the bile. A ju ju man could use it in a spell that could cause him harm or death.

And too, he was tense with anticipation. Mpanda had told them that tomorrow would start the final battle to kill all of the hated Zakariya. It was not that he was a coward. He carried his badge of courage with him always in the form of his withered right leg. His secret clan name was Scar, because of the marks left by the leopard many years ago. He had not killed the beast. It had gotten away. But his fame was born in the fact that he had recovered refusing the missionary's medicine that sapped the strength of fighting men.

Recently, he had proved himself again when they ambushed the red hats, dressed in their strange mottled clothes like the skins of tree snakes. The young white chief's heart had gone to Mpanda, as was the leader's due. But, because of his bravery, Hlobane had been given the honor of the dead man's liver.

It was not cowardice, then. Hlobane knew and trusted his sword and spear. But the rifle that had been given him was a frightening puzzlement. It became alive in his hands, full of powerful spirits. But they were foreign spirits, far from home, and Hlobane did not know the proper offerings to mollify them and keep them friendly.

He was also disturbed by the woman who lay tight against him, naked arms and legs wrapped tightly around him, snoring softly. It was bad enough that women were allowed to fight with the warriors, neglecting their assigned tasks. But he knew if he moved, she would awaken and demand to mate with him yet again. She was not unattractive with her tribal scarred cheeks, even though Hlobane preferred his women fat and soft. It was just not proper to lie with a woman so close to battle. Women sucked the strength of men, and he had not time to properly purify himself.

And last, of course, was the pain in his groin caused by his full bladder. That uneasiness, at least, he could relieve soon. He could feel the woman's grip lessen as she sank deeper into sleep. Soon now he would free himself and spill his water behind the wooden boxes. Then maybe he could rest.

Chatham checked his watch again. It was 0400. There was nothing left to do but wait. He had rechecked the men's positions while he passed the word to be near shelter. He was satisfied. The one M-60 he had placed in the center of the firing line by him, with the widest field of fire. The two grenadiers were at the end of the wings. All but two of the riflemen were strung out behind the natural barricade on the fringe of the ruin. The other two were to engage target of opportunity while protecting against flanking movements.

Blair was with Chatham. Chatham would have use of him at sunup. Freddy was there, too, because Chatham couldn't think of where else to place him. He had been quiet, maybe due to exhaustion, but had followed orders without question. He knew he wouldn't have to be looking for Mhlangana. The rebel leader would be coming to them directly. Elana was behind a shattered stone pillar in the rubble several paces behind him.

After the final instructions, Chatham squatted behind the cracked granite block and undid the latches of the rifle case that he had carried from the river.

"No change," Blair said, his eyes masked by the night glasses. "Except most of the fires are out." He had good eyes. With the moon and firelight gone, Chatham couldn't make out a damn thing in the camp.

He flipped open the case and lifted the rifle out

of its foam rubber nest. The XM-21 was an accurized M-14 semiautomatic. It had been almost completely rebuilt from stock, having match sights, star gauged barrel and glass bedded stock. He had first been introduced to this specialized man-killer at the Army Marksmanship Training Unit at Ft. Benning.

Next, he took out the Sionics sound suppressor from its slot and carefully threaded it to the muzzle. It was over a foot long and added considerably to the weight. You can't completely silence a weapon firing a supersonic bullet. The missile creates a sound wave and the sonic boom cracks against any object that it passes. But with all those booms going off, anyone within a 135-degree arc in front of the sniper is deceived as to the shooter's position. The resulting confusion allows more time to engage targets.

Lastly, he snapped on the 3' x 9' telescope, completing his sniper package. It wasn't an Adjustable Ranging Telescope, but it was the best he could come up with. He took out two boxes of 7.62-mm ammunition and pushed the empty case out of the way. He cradled the rifle on his lap and had just laid out the magazines for loading when the light flashed.

He ducked down in reflex behind the stone block as the shock wave and explosion followed. The painful concussion and roar of the blast rattled his clenched teeth. Debris started to rain out of the dark. They were pelted by rocks, dirt clods, and larger unidentifiable chunks. Beyond them, they could hear thumps that must have been whole tree trunks falling to earth.

He risked a look. He could see flames dimly through the dust laden air. Secondary explosions started going off as small arms ammunition and mortar rounds were ignited.

"Well, well, well," Blair breathed in awe. "How much C-four was in your homemade little bomb, anyway?"

"Enough to even the odds a little, I hope."

Secondary explosions had continued for an hour before silence returned. Comparative silence, for they could still hear faint screams and calls for help. But it wasn't until the sun came up that they could see the extent of the damage.

Trees were flattened, splintered, or leaning at acute angles in a large area gouged out of the jungle. It was a moonscape of craters and trenches where tons of earth had been torn up. Smoke from smoldering wood and dust hung in a pall.

At first, in the early golden light, they could see nothing moving. Chatham knew that even that gigantic explosion couldn't have eliminated the whole rebel force. Then, slowly, small groups dazedly began to crawl over the mounds and pits searching for equipment or comrades. The less courageous followed when nothing happened to the first. The smoking ruins of the forest looked like an ant nest trod on by the feet of gods.

"Describe Mhlangana, again," Chatham said to Elana, scanning the growing crowd with binoculars.

"He was a good six feet and built like a rugby forward. He was shaved bald. But the easiest thing to spot is the camouflage suit he's wearing. The only one I saw in camp. He boasted that it was taken from one of the first mercs they caught."

"I can't count on that. He could have taken it off. And he might have been in his deserted love nest when the sky caved in. I wished to hell I knew one way or another. But I can't wait any longer. We've got a train to catch. Let's get to work." Chatham handed the glasses to Blair. "We'll start on the first targets that present themselves."

Blair was Chatham's spotter. He hadn't had enough time with the rifle at the range. He had hurriedly tried to zero it in for five hundred meters and it was pretty well on. But his first shots would be made at well over one thousand. Kentucky windage would be involved. Blair, with the binocular's wider field, would pick the targets and let him know where his rounds were hitting.

He lay prone, the forestock resting on an improvised sandbag in a notch between two boulders, and fitted the stock to his shoulder, wrapping the sling around his left forearm.

"Okay, let's have the first one."

The clan leaders would be easy to find. The tribesmen, after observing those wielding power, had decided that the badge of rank was a white shirt. Every rebel leader wore one. The whiteness had long since fled from the rags, but they still made an easy bull. If Chatham could take out enough of them, the confused cannon fodder would make easier prey.

"To the left, ten o'clock, by the shattered tree."

Chatham spotted the tree, then nestled into the cheekpiece, swinging the barrel into alignment as he sighted through the scope. He skimmed over the crowd, hunting the target. He didn't find him, but stopped short and swung back.

"New target," he barked. "Wearing a headband of white feathers and red sash." Without looking, he knew Blair was quickly making the correction, trying to find the mark.

"Got him. Who the hell is that little man, anyway? Got no white shirt."

"That is Hamuraba. Grand High Wizard of the Liberation Army. Adviser to kings and cabbages. Mark it."

The witchman was making it easy, standing stationary in three-quarter profile, talking to some tribesmen digging in the dirt. Chatham lined up the cross hairs on the crown of his gray head. He took a deep breath, let it half out, his right thumb crooked over the stock automatically touching the accustomed spot on his cheek. He took up the slack and started to squeeze the three-pound pull of the trigger.

The stock slammed into his shoulder to the accompaniment of the clicking bolt. He was regaining his sight picture as he heard the crack of the sonic boom.

"Waist high, hair to the right."

Hamuraba had turned full face and was swiveling his head like an expectant vulture. He probably thought the ammo dump was still sounding off.

This time the black cross rested over his right shoulder above the top of his head. Chatham squeezed again and the rifle bucked. He lost sight of the target as the muzzle rose.

Blair filled him in. "He's down, chest, dead-on."

All Chatham could see through the scope were two sandaled feet sticking out of a pit and two blacks gazing down in.

"Next." He left the tableau and started searching again.

"My boy is still by the tree, twenty-five meters left."

Again an easy one, crouching. But he looked like he was going to move, so Chatham hung the cross over him and touched it off. He saw a red blossom of spray.

"Head shot, dead-on!"

"Another," Chatham said quickly, knowing that the herd would start to get restless.

"Right, fifty meters, by the mound of red dirt with the bush on top. He's moving now, to the right." He was gaining speed and Chatham let him, knowing he would reach cover before Chatham could knock him down. He reached a dirt berm, but spread-eagled himself on Chatham's side, thinking the attack was from the forest.

Chatham fired quickly, too quickly. The dirt kicked up under the man's right armpit, Blair informed the marksman. Chatham drew down again and fired as the target started to roll on his back. The heavy, jacketed slug caught him in the rib cage midway between shoulder and belt. He slumped, the red stain growing on the filthy, tattered shirt.

"He's down! At the top of the mound, looking over!"

A curious head popped up, showing just a glimpse of white-clad shoulders. Chatham fired, but just kicked dirt in his face. The head disappeared.

"Miss."

There was a long pause. The rabbits had gone to ground. Plenty of uncomprehending Indians around the bodies, but no chiefs. After several minutes, though, the clan leaders started to reappear, uncertain of what was going down.

"Far right, behind the small tree with the canvas in front. Looks like he might move."

Chatham followed the directions and saw the head. Popping out, taking a quick look and drawing back like a turtle. Chatham didn't try to line up the sights, just kept watch. Then the Mpeche bolted, scurrying toward the center. Chatham followed him, fired, missed, and squeezed off two more quick ones. The rebel somersaulted and went down, clutching his bleeding thigh. Chatham pumped one into his chest and he went limp.

Now even the Indians were taking cover, firing wildly in all directions.

Chatham laid down the heavy rifle and eased his tense shoulders. He rolled over and lit a cigarette while Blair kept watch.

"Make yourself useful, lover. Flip the switch on that infernal black box by your shapely little butt."

Elana looked at the object about the size of a

shoebox, resting beside a protecting rock.

"What is it?"

"Yours is not to reason why . . ." Chatham repri-
manded. "Radio beacon. An invitation to the
cavalry."

She removed the safety cover and flipped the
toggle switch.

"It doesn't sound like it's doing anything," she
said.

"You'd better hope it's singing its little heart
out." Chatham looked to the machine gunner on a
mound of rubble above him. "It's only sporting to
let them know where we are. Start the music."

The gunner fired at random. The tracer fingers
licked out, swallowed by puffs of dust just barely
visible. After a slight lag, his efforts brought results
in the form of ineffectual small arms fire, harmlessly out of range.

"Don't waste it," Chatham called. "Just enough
so they know we haven't gone away."

"You would have to go and shove a stick in the
wasps' nest," Blair complained.

Chatham discarded the smoke and rolled back
over. He peered through the scope. Now that the
Mpeche had discovered a source to vent their frustration on, they were boiling out of the trees urged
on by the screaming white shirts. The shirts flashed
in and out of the mass, trying to spread it into a
skirmish line. A lot of blacks were without rifles,
having abandoned or lost them in the dark when
the thunder fell on them. More than a few were
wildly firing in the air high above Chatham's team.

Whenever a shirt could reach these riflemen, they hammered them with gun butts until the firing stopped. All things considered, the shirts were doing a fairly decent job of controlling the runaways.

He didn't need a spotter now, so Blair fired up a smoke while Chatham shouldered the rifle again. The targets were moving, but they were coming almost straight ahead with very little deflection. He lost count of his shots. He had no hope of picking out Mhlangana in that crush, so there was no reason to conserve ammo. He swiveled back and forth, firing at any patch of white. Sometimes he saw them go down beneath the trampling feet, sometimes not. Blair fed him loaded magazines into his outstretched hand. When the rifle barrel was too hot to touch, there were no more magazines.

Until now, the machine gunner and Chatham were the only ones occupied, the rest of the team silent spectators. Chatham laid aside the sniper rifle and scanned the empty sky, then back down to the screaming black tide surging toward them. They were halfway there, too many to count.

"I really hate to be the one to say I told you so," Elana said mournfully, then ducked as the first lucky shot ricocheted off a nearby rock.

Spontaneous fire erupted from the enemy ranks. Most of it chewed up the ground in front of them, aiming low a common error when firing uphill.

"There's always a wet blanket at any orgy," Chatham commented to no one in particular.

He estimated the front rank to be about four hundred meters away when the mercs started firing without being told. He picked up his submachine gun, listening to the semiautomatic timed fire. The frontrunners began to collapse and disappear with increasing rapidity. Every shot was scoring in the closely packed mob. But it was like firing into a wave of water. The return fire started to rattle around them, but they were well dug in and none of the team paid much attention.

Chatham looked down the firing line to see one grenadier unlimber his M-79. It looked like a stubby, single-barrel scatter-gun, with a large pipe in place of the smooth-bore barrel. He broke open the breach and dropped in the 40-mm grenade shell. He snapped it closed and raised it at a thirty-degree angle. It bucked in his hands, and the grenade arched out and exploded deeply in the rolling mass. The shrapnel screamed out of the smoke burst flattening the men in the large kill zone.

The other flank grenadier commenced and, after several exploratory rounds, they both zeroed on the center of the assault line, lobbing the lethal antipersonnel bombs consistently in the faces of the front ranks. Gaping holes appeared as the riflemen continued to hammer away.

Several meters away, one of the mercs caught a round and dropped his face into the dirt. Chatham saw Elana scramble to his side, check him, then pick up his rifle and take up where he left off.

The sky was still deserted.

In 1848, at the battle of Omduran, the British—with twenty machine guns and repeating rifles—

took on forty thousand of the Mahadi's fanatic dervishes. They killed or wounded twenty thousand and broke the self-proclaimed prophet's back with a loss of only five hundred tommies. If Mhlangana was only one tenth as efficient as the other African, Chatham's farm would be bought and paid for this day.

One hundred meters separated them. The grenadiers were firing point-blank and the riflemen switched to full auto.

Chatham bent over the small generators in the tangle of wires at his feet. He picked up the one on the right and triggered it. A Claymore mine detonated in the path of the advancing horde. The shaped charge scythed down men like weeds as it sprayed out hundreds of steel pellets. Before the warriors could recover, he triggered the next firing device. And another. And another. Always in the faces of the front Mpeche.

The line shuddered and lost momentum. Fifty meters from the mercs and the main body stalled out. But individual warriors caught the battle frenzy and kept moving. They were oblivious to their comrades who milled around leaderless, taking intense fire, then rolling back slowly. Freddy, Blair, and Chatham engaged the berserkers while the rest continued to mangle the main force.

They cut down the heroes. Chatham caught one full in the chest from about ten feet, realizing in passing that it had been a woman.

Then, popping up in front, three warriors broke over the lip of the barricade and were among the whites. Chatham lost track of the raging battle around him, reflex hand-to-hand creating tunnel vision.

One black landed straddling Chatham and swung viciously with his *seme*. Chatham caught the blade with the submachine gun silencer that bent out of true but trapped and held the sword. The Mpeche struggled to free it as Chatham's right hand streaked out. Chatham stabbed his stiffened fingers into his throat.

Before the warrior could topple, his corpse shuddered and Chatham felt wetness on his own belly. He shoved the dead weight off and saw Elana over the smoking rifle barrel, a wild look in her eye. The wetness was his late enemy's blood that had gushed out of the ruin of his back.

The other two invaders were down as well. Chatham didn't know who wasted them. He scrambled back to his feet, eyes front, ignoring his now useless submachine gun.

They hadn't been overrun but they were still dead men. The team was only meant as a diversion, and once the black steamroller got hyped-up again, they would be squashed like a gnat. The rebels hadn't even retreated to the tree line, but were re-forming in the center of the clearing. Chatham tried to think of some stirring last words.

Then thoughts of his fragile mortality were wafted out of his head by whirling rotors. The howling of the Mpeche and the gunfire were drowned out by the noise of the choppers until they were almost directly overhead, flying down the throats of the panicking tribesmen.

The gunships made strafing runs with rockets and machine guns working overtime, one after another. Great rents appeared in the packed throng. Bodies disintegrated as the high explosive slammed into the stony soil, deflecting the blasts back into flesh. The terrified natives couldn't stand up to it. The Mpeche force split apart like a starburst and fled.

Then the air was thick with locust swarms of troop ships that disgorged the 2nd onto the vacated clearing, amid the enemy bodies. High above, the command ship directed the units in a coordinated counterattack.

Chatham sat back and lit a cigarette, drawing the smoke through his dry throat into his lungs.

"Lord protect us from ye of little faith," he said softly.

The clearing was crowded with the motionless helicopters and the rattle of gunfire was far away. The eight survivors of the team and Chatham rested in the shade in the deserted camp. Roving security patrols collected the bodies littering the area and dumped them in a central location. They methodically disposed of the wounded and added them to the collection.

It was 0800 and Chatham was just about to gather the British agents and get moving again. Then the CO of the security detail approached, followed by five tiger-suited men. The one in the middle was big and black and had his hands bound behind him. Chatham moved to meet them, Elana and Freddy tailing him and catching up as he met the group.

"We found him pinned under a tree limb," the officer explained. "That's how he got the gash in the head. Said he's been there ever since the explosion. He asked to speak to the commander. I thought you might be interested, so I didn't kill him."

"Yes, thank you, Captain. I'll take care of him."

The officer led his men away. Chatham looked at Elana and she nodded.

"Mr. Frederic Basil Baden-Balfour, may I present General Mpanda Mhlangana. The pleasure is all ours, General."

It's tough to look regal in dirty, torn fatigues and a blood encrusted face, but he managed just fine. He was dark, almost iridescent purple, with a flat nose and high imposing forehead. Fire still burned in his eyes and he stood proud and tall.

He ignored Chatham as a monarch would ignore a chamberpot orderly and spoke to Freddy in fluent but strangely accented English.

"I recognize your name, outlander," he rumbled majestically. Yes sir, a fine figure of a man. "You expressed a desire to speak with me concerning certain matters. If you will be good enough to remove these bonds, and adjourn to the shade, it would greatly facilitate the discussion."

Freddy began to speak but Chatham cut him off with a gesture.

"You were a very dangerous man, Mhlangana."

"I still am, mercenary."

"No, you are a prisoner, nothing more. And before that, you were the unwitting prisoner of others."

His eyes glowered but his voice was still cool and scornful. "Are meaningless taunts your only weapon, jackal?"

"Oh, by no means meaningless. A certain comrade-in-arms, Hamuraba, was the most powerful witchman in your army, I understand."

"In some ways my tribesmen are still children. Especially in their religious beliefs. Comrade Hamuraba was an educated man who trained by my side in China. He took the guise of ju ju man to bolster the courage of my people. He was my trusted advisor, second only to me in power."

"Exactly. And a traitor."

"Your lies mean nothing to me."

"The truth, Mhlangana. You were blind. Hamuraba was in league with Tashfin, himself. It was Hamuraba's idea to kidnap Miss Christian, wasn't it?"

"Yes and it was a good plan."

"Except that it was conceived by the Field Marshal. Two days before your raid, Hamuraba was driven by Tashfin's aide in his personal limousine to the dock in Lamapur, and a government launch took him upriver. That's when he suggested the raid to you. Before you attacked, Tashfin made sure that the hotel was guarded by troops that were sure to run."

"And why would Tashfin and Hamuraba conspire thus?"

"Hamuraba knew which side would win, so he joined up. As for Tashfin, it provided him with two opportunities to kill you. It's my bet that he had an ambush in the works for you in the city, but you moved too fast for him to spring it. But in case you did succeed, I was his trump card.

"He asked me to kill you once before and I refused. Tashfin believed that I would undertake the mission if I had more of a personal interest. So he gave you Miss Christian for bait."

"Prove this to me!" the black demanded, his voice tight with rage. "You have no proof!"

"I don't have to prove anything. You couldn't command a three-year-old child now.

"There is a game of nations continually being played. Powerful nations sit together, making moves and countermoves in a chess game with dozens of participants. Nobody wants to win so much as they don't want to lose. Their aim, if in fact they have one, is to perpetuate the game. Nonplayers are dangerous only when they threaten to kick over the table—and have the means to do so.

"Your army is in the process of being ground to dust. And with it, your power. You are no longer dangerous. Much worse, perhaps, you are now merely useless."

Mhlangana began his retort, but the sneer melted from his lips, and the supercilious look was first replaced by amazement and finally fear.

Chatham leveled the S&W and shot him three times in the chest.

He stood with Blair in the dustcloud kicked up

by the Westland Scout. He shouted over the whine of the turbine and rotors.

"The commanders have their orders to pursue and maintain contact with the rebels until nightfall, at least. They will advance to the river, then sweep north and south. I have ordered most of the helicopters back to the field. You and the members of the strikeforce can ride back if you wish, but I would prefer you remain here and keep an eye on things for me."

"Right, Boss," he grinned. "I'll hang around with the boys until you get back."

Chatham was relieved. He had hoped he could keep Blair out of any possible fighting in the capital when von Heydeck rolled in. He made his farewells and climbed in the chopper.

He settled into the back seat of the light aircraft with Elana and Freddy. He picked up the headphones and mike.

"Take her up, Captain, and pour on the coals. I want to be at the river mouth as soon as possible."

The helmeted pilot gave thumbs up, nodded to the copilot, and twisted the throttle lever. They rose, turned on their axis, and were thrust forward by the jet engine. They were over the river and headed for the sea in minutes.

Chatham put the headphone on but switched off the mike. It was the first time that Freddy had the chance to speak to him alone, and he didn't waste time.

"I thought I could trust you," he moaned and snarled across Elana. "You had it planned all along to destroy the rebels, didn't you? While feeding me that line about opening negotiations!"

"I know. And it's all the more terrible since you were always so straightforward and honest with me," Chatham commented dryly.

Freddy's complexion started to purple, so he went on. "But what's the big problem? Mhlangana, by your own admission, was your second choice to head the government. How about if I arrange for the first string to take over?"

Puzzled, Freddy asked, "You mean al-Kumi? But he isn't strong enough to overthrow Tashfin. That was the whole problem."

"And what if Tashfin was removed? No rebels, no dictator. Just a deserted field left open for the first taker."

It started to dawn on him. "You haven't finished then? You mean the boat . . ."

". . . isn't just my means of escape. I have a better use for it first."

Freddy settled back in his seat to fully digest the new developments. Chatham gazed out the front canopy, looking for the blue of the sea.

The MBT was right where it was supposed to be, moored at the river mouth. The pilot circled it once. The streamlined craft, seventy-three feet long, painted gray, was stripped of the torpedo tubes that it was designed to carry. The motor torpedo boat retained the twin 20-mm cannon tub on the deck forward of the cockpit and the .50-calibers on each side. On the rear deck, Chatham could make out a swing turret-mounted combination 81-mm mortar and .50-caliber. Several crewmen moved about on the deck and a Ma'ribassan naval flag fluttered fitfully from the stern flagstaff.

Chatham switched the mike on. "That's the MBT, Captain. Take us down."

The pilot was good. He kept the chopper hovering five feet over the bow. Freddy jumped first. Then, with the help of two crewmen, caught Elana. Chatham was the last one on the deck. The pilot waved, gained altitude and headed north. Chatham watched him until he was out of sight, then followed Freddy to the cockpit.

There were several officers on the bridge in navy khaki. The giant, wrinkled skipper turned from the wheel as they approached and acknowledged them with a terse nod.

"Colonel Chatham, Commander O'Donnel of the Royal Navy."

"Hello, Commander, glad you could make it."

"My pleasure, Colonel. About the only action I get nowadays is with you clandestine chaps," he replied with a stone face.

"Are the commandos aboard?"

"Yes. Been below decks since we left Micramar before dawn."

"Fine. Set the course for the mouth of the Northern Kasambi. Think we can make it by noon?"

"Easily, Colonel. The twin twelve-seventy-one power plants have been reworked by government marine engineers. Instead of twenty-seven knots, this little darling will do fifty. We'll be there with time to spare."

"All right. Freddy, you know the infiltration point. Show it to the Commander on the charts. I want to have a look at the marines."

Chatham was satisfied with the Royal Marine Commando detachment. The rifle squad, outfitted in sanitized equipment, although sweating and uncomfortable from the airless, confined quarters, was fit and ready to go. He closed the hatch to their forward compartment and stepped into the smaller quarters under the bridge. The roar of the beefed-up engines running close to full throttle permeated everywhere.

"What does a girl have to do to get a little privacy around here?" Elana asked from her seat on the miniscule bunk, her overalls bunched around her tiny waist. She paused in the midst of sponging off her dirty shoulders and breasts with a bucket of sea water. "Every time I try to scrub some of the grime off my lily-white body, another sneaky Pete pops up."

"Blame it on your animal magnetism."

"Yes, and look where it's gotten me so far. In a love nest with a candid, simple soldier of fortune, who isn't, and raped in a grass shack by a native strongman, who surely wasn't, in spades. Pardon the pun."

"You seem to have fully recovered from your misfortunes."

"You can't keep a good spy down. They were very thorough at training school. There were some classes I got straight A's in. Natural aptitude."

"I'll pen a testimonial to that effect."

"What did you excel in at your training school?"

"Beg pardon?"

"Come, come, Erik sweet. Don't try to pull one over me after all we've meant to each other. You may be just a hard-as-nails mercenary to Freddy, but I know better."

"You're making my head spin, lover."

"Okay, we'll play it that way. You said you knew I was a British agent from the start. Then you knew that I was going to bed with you because I was ordered to." She paused at Chatham's mock horrified expression. "And don't give me that old act either. All of which means that you didn't come charging into the jaws of the rebel army to save your beloved. You had some reason of your own. The same reason that you risked that foray into the camp alone. You came to kill Mhlangana, not rescue me.

"And now you're on your way to kill Tashfin. Remind me never to get on the wrong side of you. It appears to me that you are a very specialized technician. And I don't think the local gangsters can afford you. Knock out the free enterprise and you're left with government hi-jinks. Cross out the Communists: they had to put their money on the People's Liberation Army, like it or not. I'm banking that your leash ends up in the hands of the CIA."

She was smart as well as dangerous, it seemed. She had missed a few angles, though. The best place to terminate Tashfin and still have hope of getting clear was when he sailed down to meet the arms shipment. That meant Chatham had to use the coastal gun emplacement and its equipment. But it was occupied by a company of paras who were still on Tashfin's payroll. When Tashfin got tricky with the kidnapping, he gave Chatham the chance to get the whole 2nd Regiment buried safely in the boonies.

The torpedo boat must have hit a wicked sea swell. It shuddered, then leaped forward, tossing Chatham on top of Elana. They both sprawled on the bunk.

"Looks like they taught you a few commendable techniques, too," she said softly in his ear. "Remember when I said I wouldn't see you again because my admiration might turn to love?" He nodded and she smiled impishly. "Now that I know you are just as devious and rotten as I am, there's no question of uncontrollable admiration. I think we were made for each other, honey."

He gave her a hard, deep kiss and, as she arched into him, he got to his feet. "I hate to leave just when the topic of discussion was getting interesting. But I think I hear my mother calling."

"All right for now. Try not to let her blow your scheming ass off."

He blew her a kiss and went topside.

"The tide is out, Colonel. I make it about one thousand meters of tidal flat." Commander O'Donnel stood with the binoculars hanging unused around his neck.

"How close can you get us?"

"The bottom falls out of the shelf just about at the waterline. I can nudge the bow into the mud if I don't push it. The incoming tide should have us afloat by the time you return. But that's still quite a hike."

"But necessary. The only time the shore is unguarded is when the tide's out. Company C has left a few guards at the emplacement."

Chatham went to the stern deck to check the five commandos one last time. Freddy handed him a Swedish K machine pistol.

"You're not going along on this one, too?"

"Yes I am. Somebody has to keep an eye on you." He was still surly around the edges.

"Up to you," Chatham shrugged. "If any of us gets wasted or captured, it's no loss. But Her Majesty's Government would choke on explaining just what the Undersecretary of the British Legation was doing with his pants down. Like I said, suit yourself."

The power plants idled back as Chatham finished the inspection, and, soon after, they cut out altogether. There was a slight bump as the bow ran aground into the mud.

The MBT crewmen lowered a rope ladder from the bow. Chatham was the first down. He sank knee-deep in mud and armpit-deep in sea water. It was a fight to keep from drowning until he fought clear of the water. He waited for the others, then they all started for the shore of the peninsula.

The vile-smelling mud fought them like something alive, clutching at their legs, tripping them so that they were soon coated with it. It obliterated both camouflage fatigues and body paint.

A third of the way there and already their lungs burned and muscles screamed. Chatham looked over his shoulder between gasps. Everyone was keeping together pretty well, except for Freddy. He lagged so far behind and fell so often, it looked as if he was trying to crawl in. No one dropped out to help. He knew that before he dealt himself in.

When they reached the rocks at the base of the cliff, Chatham called a five-minute halt. It was an easy climb to the top; he knew that from his trip with Elana. But he doubted if they could have made it right then. The men cleaned their weapons and when they did reach the top after the break Freddy was still struggling through the flats below.

They moved through the trees and halted on the rise looking down on the bunker. The squad leader, a burly Scots sergeant, and Chatham crawled to the ridge.

A sentry paced along the length of the landward side of the concrete structure. Chatham timed two trips. He was out of sight behind the far end for about two minutes each time.

When he started the third, Chatham said to the sergeant, "When the merc's out of sight, I'll make my run. It will be close. If the sentry sees me, waste him. Then I'll have to try to get inside before they button up and get on the wireless." He slung the

machine pistol on his back and took his garrote wire
from his pocket.

The sentry disappeared and Chatham was up
and running. The down slope was steeper than he
gauged and he was soon fighting to keep one lead-
heavy leg in front of the other to avoid sprawling on
his face. Then he was dashing through the entry
lane in the barbed wire and crashing into the sun-
heated concrete wall. He fought to fill his starving
lungs and at the same time silence his heavy gasping.

Either he succeeded or the merc's heavy tread
masked it, because he passed right by Chatham. He
flipped the wire noose over the enemy's head, put
his knee in the small of his back and pulled the garrote taut. The merc went to his knees and clawed at
his neck. But the wire had bitten into the skin and
he couldn't get at it. Chatham kept it tight for a
minute after the struggling stopped, then checked
for a pulse. By that time, the rest of the commandos
were beside him. Freddy was with them, pasty-
faced and wheezing.

Chatham unlimbered the Swedish K and moved
to the steel door set in the bunker wall. It swung
easily on its hinges. He stepped inside and was at
the head of a flight of narrow metal stairs descend-
ing to another steel hatch. A metal ladder rose to
the second floor, but the hatch was padlocked shut.
They moved to the second door, weapons ready.

Chatham pushed it open cautiously and looked
through. There was a hall running the length of the
bunker, poorly lit by several bare bulbs. Conversa-

tion and laughter echoed out of an open door about ten feet to the left. The radio room, he guessed. He motioned the sergeant and several of his men to take it and took the rest with him to the right.

As he approached the first of two doors, he heard exclamations of alarm seconds before the chatter of automatic fire thundered in the enclosed space. Then the sounds of overturned furniture, smashing glass, and ricochets. Chatham pushed back his door with a clang and leaped through at an angle, leaving room for the following marine. The rest moved to the next door.

He was in the deserted gun chamber fronting the bunker. Farther down, the other door slammed open and the commandos came through. The sergeant and his crew joined them and told Chatham that the three remaining mercs had been killed and the radio smashed.

Sitting in front of the single firing port with muzzles protruding were four recoilless rifles nine feet long. The emplacement had been designed for naval cannon and its size dwarfed the rifles. The ceiling was about ten feet high and the chamber was 125 feet wide by 200 long. The open firing slot cut in the six-foot-thick walls was three feet high and ran half the length of the reinforced front.

Chatham looked out the firing aperture. There was an excellent view of the river below. No ships or boats were in sight. The tripod mounts for the rifles were built up at the rear to tilt the barrels down to cover the surface. He turned the breech lever. Next he checked the .50-caliber spotting gun mounted coaxially on top of the larger barrel by working the charging handle. All seemed to be in excellent working order.

Chatham left one of the commandos as lookout for vessels and hunted for the ammunition. The cardboard container tubes were stacked neatly in a corner, well over a hundred rounds. There were a few HEAT shells—high explosive antitank—that could play havoc with metal armor plate. But he was pleased to see that the greatest majority were HEP-T: high explosive plastic with tracer cartridge. It was designed for tank armor, also. On impact with the turret, the plastic filler spreads out like putty. Almost instantaneously, the detonator sets it off and the shockwaves cause chipping of the interior surfaces. You kill off the enemy crew and take possession of a slightly used tank. It is also very effective against bunkers, personnel, and wooden structures. Like boats.

A normal gun crew is made up of a squad leader, gunner, loader, and security rifleman. Chatham was going to take over as leader and gunner, so he taught the sergeant the duties of the loader. With a little practice, he was opening the breech and loading the big shells fast and smooth. Chatham loaded the magazine into the .50. All that remained was the warning for the others to stay out of the lethal back blast area, and they sat, with what few dry cigarettes they could muster, to wait.

A little short of an hour later, almost 1300 on the dot, the lookout called Chatham to the firing slit. He leaned out, following the commando's pointing finger. Just sailing around the headland, a large freighter steamed into view, still several miles away. Chatham looked to the left, upriver, but there was no sign of the welcoming committee.

He started to get jumpy when the steamer halved the distance and still no target. If Tashfin met the ship anywhere but here all of his planning was worthless.

Again the lookout was the first to spot the three boats round a bluff a mile upriver.

They grew in size and Chatham turned angrily to Freddy. "I thought you said he would come alone?"

Freddy peered out at the launch flying the Field Marshal's pennant and the two gunboats flanking it. Their decks were loaded with troops, almost shoulder to shoulder.

"He always came alone before," Freddy fired back defensively. "He must have gotten cautious since the Second was taken away."

Chatham turned to the sergeant. "You'd better be in your best form. I'll have to knock out all three boats or they can land below and pick up off in the mud flats."

He watched the smaller craft approach. They stayed well in the center of the channel. That would put the range at about five thousand meters when they came even with the bunkers. That was no problem. The recoilless could reach out well over seven thousand with its flat trajectory.

Chatham sat down on the gunner's seat on the side of the mount and cranked the traverse wheel until the barrel stopped as far to the left as it would go. He ignored the freighter and the gunboats, intent only on Tashfin's launch.

He took the binoculars and hunted for it, found and held it. The white paint, trimmed in dark teak, sparkled in the sun. He focused the glasses. There on the flying bridge stood the dictator, all gold braid, crimson trim, and shiny medals. Beside him was faithful Faran. Various uniformed toadies crowded the stern deck, leaving little room for the white uniformed crew.

When the launch was within the limits of his field of fire, Chatham pressed his eye to the soft rubber eyepiece of the telescopic sight. He could make out the hull in the upper right of his sight picture, so he cranked the elevation wheel with his right hand and centered the launch. He moved the traverse keeping it there. The launch was larger than a tank so Chatham made the necessary mental calculations as he centered it in the reticle pattern. By the stadia lines, he estimated range at barely over five thousand.

From his angle, he could look right into the open bridge at Tashfin and his heroic posturing. He went through the firing drill for his loader's benefit.

"Fire mission. HEP."

The sergeant slammed the plastic explosive shell in the breech, closed and locked it.

"Ready!"

"Front. Boat. Five thousand. Two leads."

He made the final elevation correction and pulled the fire knob while continuing the traverse.

The .50-caliber tracer round lanced out and the white phosphorus tip exploded in a puff of white smoke on the deck at Tashfin's feet. He started to duck when Chatham pushed the firing knob in.

Chatham heard the roar and felt the pressure of the back blast. In the sight, the bridge disintegrated like balsa wood. Without waiting to get a good look at his handiwork, he deflected the gun tube on the hull slightly below the waterline.

"Fire mission." The sergeant flipped the breech lever, opening the block and ejecting the spent casing. "HEP."

"Ready!"

"Front. Boat. Five thousand. One lead."

Chatham pushed the firing knob and, with the accompanying roar, the boat was hidden by a geyser of water.

The screaming sirens made Chatham all too aware of the gunboats. He tore his eye away from the sight and located them. He cranked the wheels fast, sweat starting to roll off his forehead.

The first boat swung around and paused to return fire. It was the worst move the skipper could have made.

"Fire mission." The breech was empty and waiting. "HEAT."

"Ready!"

He skipped the fire drill, filled the reticle with the bow gun. It fired. He ignored the blast as its shell hit low on the emplacement and hit the firing knob once more.

Chatham's shell must have hit the forward ammunition magazine because the whole bow disappeared in a blinding flash.

Again, Chatham looked up to scan the water. The second gunboat commander was smarter than his mate. He was already close to the shore, beneath the field of fire. The troops were running to the bow, preparing to land.

"That's it. Let's get out of here," Chatham ordered.

He paused for one last look.

The crewmen of the freighter were crowding the rail gaping at the unexpected tableau. The launch was dead in the water, settling fast with a gaping hole in its side and only jagged wood in place of the bridge. The wreck of the gunboat was obscured by the oily, black smoke belching from it. Heads of those passengers lucky enough to be alive bobbed in the water around the hulks.

Chatham caught up with the others in the sunlight in the entrance. They stripped themselves of unnecessary gear and started the run for the cliffs. The pursuing troops had a long hard climb up the bluffs, but the commandos had the mud to cross. The race would be pretty even.

They were all gasping when they got to the cliffs. Still, they careened from rock to rock on the descent, trusting in fate to keep from breaking their necks.

The tide had risen, but not much. The MBT sat idling in the water, helpless to close the gauntlet.

They started churning through the muck.

The blood was pounding in Chatham's ears and

his ragged breath was tearing his lungs apart. He didn't hear the firing, only saw the mud erupt around him. He sprawled on his back and saw the tiny figures on the cliff top firing their toy guns. One figure at the end of the line lay still in the mud. Chatham didn't know how he knew it was Freddy beneath the coat of mud, but he did.

Chatham motioned the others past him, then flopped back to Freddy. Chatham didn't ask where or even if he was hit when he reached him. Chatham had no breath left for words. And it really didn't matter if Freddy was mortally wounded or if he was just tired. He knew the rules.

With awkwardness born of exhaustion, Chatham tossed his machine pistol at Freddy. It landed in the mud near him, and his arm snaked out and drew it to him.

"You slippery son-of-a-bitch," he gasped. "I hope you burn in everlasting hell." His white grin was centered in the black muck covering his face.

As Chatham turned to half crawl, half swim toward salvation, he saw Freddy swearing at the clogged breech of the weapon, trying to clear it with grimy hands. He never got the chance to use it. The next volley from shore stitched him and the surrounding mire full of holes. So much for Chatham's one beau geste.

He would most likely have been the next unfortunate target, except that the government troops were considerably distracted.

The torpedo boat's twin 20-mm cannons opened up, raking the cliff top. The enemy sought cover behind large boulders at the brink that even the cannons couldn't pierce. But that wasn't the intention. From the stern, the mortar began to cough its deadly aerial bombs. Several bracketing rounds fell short, then one overshot. Then the mortarmen found the range and death began to rain relentlessly. The boulders screened the number of dead and wounded. But when the troops retreated, there were very few of them.

Chatham staggered the remaining distance, was lifted aboard and lay gasping on the deck as the high-speed boat roared out to sea.

By the time the raiders had recovered, they were well on their way to international waters. Chatham had one last duty and lurched below with Elana to the radio room. With shaking hands, he set the dials and keyed the mike.

"Red Wings. I say again, Red Wings. Over."

He stared at the speaker, willing it to respond, but only static muttered back at him.

"Red Wings. I say again, Red Wings. Over."

Faintly there was a change in the hissing pattern and he leaned forward to wring the words out.

"Black Ribbon. I say again, Black Ribbon. Over."

He put down the mike and rested his forehead on the cool steel radio table. He woke up later in a bunk, minus mud-caked clothes. He didn't know who moved him or when.

Chatham sat, comfortable and carefree, basking in air-conditioned luxury in the U.S. Consulate. Why shouldn't he be without care? The passport in his pocket said that he was James Brookes, successful businessman, and entry stamps attested that he had entered the country legally two days ago for a well-deserved holiday. Actually, when he had crossed the Kenyan border the night before, he was still Erik Chatham, fugitive deserter and assassin. It's amazing the wonders wrought by a good night's rest in a Company safe house in Nairobi.

"The Executive Secretary to the Consul General will see you now, Mr. Brookes."

He returned the brilliant plastic smile of the receptionist and got up from the easy chair. He smoothed his spotless tropical weight suit and crossed the thick wine red carpet. He caught her green-eyed look at his tan. Cattily thinking how nice it was to have long hours of leisure to spend under a sun lamp when poor girls had to work for a living.

He closed the dark wood double doors that reached all the way to the ten-foot ceiling and sat in the leather lounge chair facing the desk. Visible across it, over an expanse big enough to land a fighter on, sat a gentleman with all the caste marks of a Company CT: a career trainee. In his late thirties, he was well into his full twenty-year stint. With his light suit, carefully cropped, iron-gray hair, manicured, slender white fingers, and an aristocratic face, he reminded Chatham a little of Tashfin.

"Mr. Chatham, my name is Henry Bassey, and I have been instructed to convey to you congratulations on a job well done. Especially because the considerable expense involved was incurred by one of our most esteemed allies.

"I am allowed to inform you further that within the past few days, a deplorable totalitarian dictatorship has been deposed by a democratic, enlightened leader in the sovereign nation of Ma'ribassa. In an unheralded display of support and solidarity, the people of this nation banded together and condemned the Communist agitators for the blatant foreign agents that they were. The virtually bloodless power shift was facilitated by the loyal units of the Third Volunteer Territorial Paracommandos who invested the capital in the name of the world renowned statesman, Mr. al-Kumi."

It was pathetic. He actually believed half of the bullshit that he was given to recite.

"Unfortunately, the revolution was not without some casualties. Among them the fascist strongman, Field Marshal of the dissident armed forces, who was murdered by traitorous officers of his own staff. Also, by coincidence, a junior officer of the British diplomatic community suffered a heart attack and died while pleasure cruising off the coast."

"To make an omelet . . ." Chatham ventured.

"Exactly, exactly," Henry hurriedly cut in. Chatham got the feeling that his presence made the CT exceedingly nervous. Like he would blow his nose in the table linen.

"Well, as I said when you contacted us, the Consulate is more than happy to render any assistance possible to its citizens abroad. I have your tickets for tonight's flight to New York, via Rome and London, as you requested. I have also taken the liberty of seeing that a limousine picks you up at your hotel to take you to the airport. Shall we say around eight o'clock then?"

"No."

"I beg your pardon?"

"You have been so much help to me already, I know you won't mind changing my reservations to next week. Circumstances have changed since last night, and I really haven't had a chance to see some local sights as much as I would have liked."

His voice stiffened. "It was my impression, Mr. Chatham, that your firm requested your presence as soon as possible to lecture on your recent travels."

"Mr. Bassey, please." The CT blushed. "I rather think that they can go on saving the world for freedom without me for another week."

"This is highly irregular," he sniffed.

"I'm in a highly irregular line of work." Chatham got up to leave. "This wasn't really covered in your instructions, was it? Try adlibbing once. You may get to enjoy it. See you next week, Henry."

Once in his hotel room, Chatham got rid of the coat and tie. He adjusted the air-conditioning and fixed himself a scotch poured into an ice-filled glass, then walked into the bedroom.

The naked girl on the bed rolled over on her back and gave a feline stretch.

"It's about time," Elana said. "I thought you

were going to talk with those politicians all day."

He smiled and set the glass down, untouched. It was a shame. The ice had long since melted by the time he got back to it.

Action And Adventure From The World Famous EDGAR RICE BURROUGHS

CHARTER BOOKS
Suspense to Keep You
On the Edge of Your Seat